The Dodo Knight

The Dodo Knight

by Michelle Rene

AnnorlundaBooks

Dedicated to my son.

Contents

A boat beneath a sunny sky,
Lingering onward dreamily
In an evening of July —

Children three that nestle near,
Eager eye and willing ear,
Pleased a simple tale to hear —

Long has paled that sunny sky:
Echoes fade and memories die:
Autumn frosts have slain July.

Still she haunts me, phantomwise,
Alice moving under skies
Never seen by waking eyes.

Children yet, the tale to hear,
Eager eye and willing ear,
Lovingly shall nestle near.

In a Wonderland they lie,
Dreaming as the days go by,
Dreaming as the summers die:

Ever drifting down the stream —
Lingering in the golden gleam —
Life, what is it but a dream?

-Lewis Carroll.

Prologue

I have it on very good authority that a muse must have their heart broken six times before they can die. Apparently, they are mortally indestructible before such time as a deep hurt or ache penetrates their heart six times. Some people can withstand only one such occurrence before they crumble. Others might be able to withstand a dozen torments. There is a story of one woman with many children, who required more than fifty such trials before she let go. That woman was one hundred and one years, five months and a day when she finally passed away. Poor dear.

The reason why muses require six breakings is not clear to me. I did not make up the silly rule, and it is a silly rule in my opinion. It just is as someone set it about. Perhaps it was God or the Devil, who knows. If the whole thing were up to me, I would make sure no one was forced to endure such terrors as these. Well, that is not completely honest. The scoundrels of the world could have their trials, but the good, honest people should be rid of them, so says I.

Of course, that becomes complicated, does it not? Deciding who is honest and who is a scoundrel. Who will choose? Heresy or no, I could tell you the just from the evil. I often find myself able to make an accurate assessment of most people I meet ten minutes into a cup of tea with them. It is a gift to which I have no real outlet other than to amuse myself, so why not use it for a real purpose?

And just who am I to make such decrees? Well, I was once a muse. I am no longer, of course. The funny thing about existing as a muse is that you rarely know you are doing so until after the fact. But once, in my gilded youth, I was a muse for a creative man far too lovely for this world.

When truly creative souls try to exist in this horrid world of ours, they rarely make it much past childhood. Most children are lovely and creative and open to the possibilities of the wide world of fantasy and whimsy. As they grow, most of that is beaten down by figures and facts, and the world itself tells everyone that there is no real place for nonsense.

Every now and again, someone will breach the wall and light our tranquil, dull lives with the lamp fire of loveliness. Alliteration aside, their souls are so unique and beautiful that we are in awe of what they can create, and what they create could last lifetimes. Such souls are rarely understood and often criticized, as is usually the plight of the truly artistic.

I had the rare opportunity to know such a soul. He

drifted in like a morning breeze and has lingered always on the periphery of my life. I was his little muse, and he was my friend. No, he was my Dodo, my Mr. Do-do-Dodgson. Most of the waking world knew him as Lewis Carroll.

Who are you, you might inquire? It seems I have been asked that question over and over again by so many. For the past several decades, my answer to that would have been, "I am Mrs. Hargreaves." Still do not know me? No, I should think not. No one of consequence knows Mrs. Hargreaves as much other than an old widow, shut away in her house. Perhaps the children nearby think me a witch by now. I certainly hope they do.

Who are you? There it is again. Such a rude question, is it not? When my Dodo knew me, that answer was so very simple. And the answer, oh the answer gives me away, I think. Perhaps too soon? I will have to tell someday, will I not? I have been hiding for so long, the real story of what happened me, to all of us.

Who are you? The question doth persist, like a pesky fly I cannot seem to swat away. All right, I suppose I must be open and honest. After all, without honesty now, what is the point of doing this at all? You will know me most assuredly by my answer when the caterpillar asked me that very same question.

"Who are you?" said the Caterpillar after removing the hookah from his mouth.

I shall offer the courtesy now that I never did with the

actual caterpillar. He never was given my name, but I doubt he really ever cared to know it. Such is the manner of caterpillars.

"Why, I am Alice, of course."

Chapter One

It was in late February of 1856 that we moved to our new home at Oxford. My father had been assigned a position as dean of Christ Church College, and we were to live in the lavish deanery on the campus grounds. My fondest memories were of that place, and still the mixed scent of old, yellowed pages with freshly trimmed gardens will recall the whimsy of my childhood. It is curious what might bring one back to a time and place in their history. I would always wrap myself up in the smells of libraries and gardens as though they were a warm blanket.

I had heard of Mr. Dodgson, of course, before we had been there long. My cousin Fredrika boasted that she had been sketched by "the most handsome and clever Mr. Dodgson", and my older brother Harry had gone out a few times rowing with the man. Harry was young and not yet skilled at the task, and Mr. Dodgson was kind enough to offer him lessons shortly after we had arrived on campus.

Harry and Fredrika told me much about Mr. Dodgson. Apparently, he was the cleverest man they had ever met.

He actually liked to talk to children, a concept most of the adults I knew were not fond of. At least, it seemed that way. Surely Mother would dote over the babies, but I often caused her an uproar as I was supposed to be silent and well behaved, a chore I found challenging at times.

"Do your lessons. Sit up straight. Do not pout so. Desist that annoying prattle, Alice."

As soon as Mother employed Miss Prickett, our governess, she let her do the meddling while Mother took to the care of the house and garden. This seemed to relax her more, and she was more able to apply kind words to us since Miss Prickett was present for the discipline.

However, none of Mother's kindness, even on her more spirited days, equaled that of the rumors of Mr. Dodgson. Harry and Fredrika both spoke of games he manufactured himself or riddles he had ready for them every outing.

I saw Mr. Dodgson once before I actually met him in the spring. He was with a man about his age, perhaps a little younger, and they were standing before the Christ Church Cathedral with a box on stilts draped in a large cape. Later, I learned that this was a camera. At the time, I was completely befuddled by the scene.

Mr. Dodgson in his professor robes flipped up the cape and hid beneath it like Ina and I did to Father's robes when we were playing. He seemed to be fiddling around with something underneath, begging the younger man posing by the cathedral to hold perfectly still. I thought both men to be of a curious sort and continued to walk alongside

Miss Prickett to avoid a good scolding, despite the urge to gawk.

Months later when the weather tuned from breezy to cold, the man came to our house and found it in a most disorderly state.

"Alice Liddell, return that teapot this instant!"

I had hidden myself away underneath the table clutching the teapot in question to my chest. It was a favorite teapot of mine with a small scene of ducks and rabbits painted on the belly. The horrid woman never used it, saying the spout poured terribly, but the instant she noticed its absence, she went on a rampage.

"Alice, where have you gone, child?"

She stomped past the table. I could see her heavy shoes beneath the table curtain as she passed. Miss Prickett was not an ugly woman, except when she was cross. By all accounts, she was handsome, with roundness in all the proper places. She had the look of a kind woman who would be warm to cuddle with on a cold day. On closer inspection, she was the type of woman who stomped like an elephant and roared when she was angry. Almost everything I did made her angry, it seemed.

I held the teapot close to me under the table. A tiny scratching sound came from within and then ceased. My body tensed, and I hoped Miss Prickett had not heard. A sudden rustling of the tablecloth spooked me, and I turned to see Edith's tiny face and wide eyes peering at me from the other side of the table.

"What you doing, Ally?"

She was only two years old at the time, so "Ally" was the only incarnation of my name she could say. I was only four, but to me and Edith, we were a world of time and knowledge apart. The tiny thing followed me everywhere.

"Hush you! I'm hiding from Pricks."

"I come too?"

"I'm not going anywhere. Just get in here before she sees you."

Little Edith smiled like a conspirator and crawled under the table with me, snuggling up to my right side. She clutched the crook of my arm.

"Do not make a sound," I whispered.

She nodded, and we huddled there together as Miss Prickett stormed past us again.

Just then, there came a rapping on the front door. Mother glided across the room to answer it, seemingly unaware of the drama playing out behind her in the dining room. She answered the door with her usual grace.

"Hello, Mr. Dodgson. Lovely to see you again. I will go tell my husband you are here," she chimed.

She floated away, leaving the man standing awkwardly in our receiving room directly across from the dining table where Edith and I hid.

I knew his name, we all did. Harry spoke of him often and his silly games. Edith perked at the sound of his name and crawled out from under the table to get a better look. I tried to grab her foot, but it was as if she had greased herself with butter. She wriggled out of my grasp and headed for the receiving room. Miss Prickett saw her, and I knew my cover was forfeit.

"Alice Liddell, are you under that table?"

She was angry, and I had one choice in the matter to avoid a scolding. I only hoped the man was as benevolent as Harry made him out to be. In a quick burst, I dashed out from beneath the table, so startling Miss Prickett that she tumbled over a nearby chair.

"Alice!" she wailed.

Not a step did I miss, even at the sound of my name. I ran through the hall, past Edith who was spying from behind a doorframe, and into the receiving room where Mr. Dodgson stood astonished. He was pristinely dressed, wearing a tall hat and crisp gray-and-black gloves. I looked into his blue eyes in a pleading way, holding up the teapot.

"Please do not let her take it," I said, nearly out of breath.

"Take what, my dear?"

"The teapot."

I lifted the lid and held it out for him to look inside. He peeked in without hesitation to see a small, brown dormouse curled into a ball among various dried sticks and grasses. The tiny thing was asleep despite the raucous all around him. Mr. Dodgson smiled.

"Alice Liddell!"

Miss Prickett burst into the room just as I replaced the lid and turned around to face her, the teapot clutched tightly to my chest. My mother was close behind her with a look of wonderment at all the commotion. Little Edith was still behind the doorframe, visibly trying not to laugh. I backed instinctively into the legs of Mr. Dodgson.

"What is happening here?" asked Mother, looking from me to Miss Prickett.

"Alice has stolen a teapot and decided to house vermin inside it," answered Miss Prickett, crossing her arms over her chest.

"Alice, what sort of business is this?"

I looked to the floor and back to my mother. "No one was using it." It was all I could manage. Vocabulary tends to leave children when they need it the most.

"Let me see," commanded Mother.

I tipped the teapot and removed the lid to show her the dormouse inside. Mother made a sour face and bade me to cover it again, but she did not seem particularly angry.

Miss Prickett looked about to burst. "I went to collect a teapot, to make the children's afternoon tea, and found this teapot hidden in Alice's bedroom with the foul rodent inside!"

Everyone looked to me again.

"She usually uses the one with the roses on it. I thought it would not be missed."

Miss Prickett scowled at me. I did not realize such a look could exist on such a young woman. I shrank back and found myself leaning into Mr. Dodgson's legs.

"If I m-m-may interject," he said shyly and with a slight stammer.

The women switched their gaze from me to him.

"Alice is just readying your t-t-teapot for latest fashion in the spring."

"She is?"

"Oh yes. Such a trend is this now in London that all fashionable houses have at least three t-t-teapots housing d-d-dormice for the winter to be ready for the spring events. The little d-d-darlings are known to leave behind in the very p-p-porcelain a spice that cannot be reprod-d-duced in any way."

Miss Prickett looked astonished, and Mother eyed Mr. Dodgson suspiciously. I turned to look back up at him, and he smiled at me with a wink.

"I had no idea such a thing even existed. Who ever heard of rodent-spiced tea?" said Miss Prickett, amazed at my apparent knowledge of fashionable trends.

"I think it's a trend b-begun in India," offered Mr. Dodgson.

The rest of us knew it was a lot of nonsense, even Mother, and I tried not to giggle. Perhaps, Miss Prickett was unaccustomed to nonsense in adults and therefore, took anything a young scholar like Mr. Dodgson said at face value. It was not a nice trick for him to play, but she did have a mind to kill my little friend in the teapot, so I reckoned one evened out the other. I was sure Mother would end the charade any moment, but she proved me wrong by letting it play itself out before her. A knowing smile was our only clue that she approved of this game.

"How did you know of such a thing, Alice?"

"I heard of it at my cousin's house. They have two teapots filled with dormice tucked away in their parlor even now. Three mice per teapot each!"

The words flowed through me as though they were truth. I wondered where they had been when I needed them moments ago.

"There, you see. Alice is only making sure your house fashionable," said Mr. Dodgson with a bit more boldness.

Miss Prickett nodded, eyes still agog.

"Miss Prickett, I believe little Edith over there is in need of a snack. In fact, we might all like a little something right now. Please see to that with the cook," said Mother mildly.

The poor, stunned governess nodded and left the room to make her way to the kitchen. Mother turned back to us.

"My husband will receive you in his study, Mr. Dodgson," she said then looked directly at me. "And I expect that teapot to be scrubbed clean as soon as the mouse has vacated. Do you understand, Alice?"

I nodded.

"You are not frightened, Mrs. Liddell?" asked Mr.

Dodgson. His upper lip quivered with the effort of concealing a stammer.

"Sir, with all due respect, I have four children, two before Alice. It would take a lot more than a rodent in a teapot to startle me," she said with a smile before she left the room.

He smiled at her, looking impressed.

As soon as she exited the room, I turned my attention to Mr. Dodgson. "Thank you."

"For what?" he asked, kneeling down to be closer to my height.

"For lying so that I might keep him."

"It is not a total lie. I am sure somewhere in the wide world there is a place that considers rodent-spiced tea to be all the rage. You are just ahead of what is fashionable."

He patted my head. It was a curious thing. I remember noticing it even then. The shy way he spoke, and that awful stammer of his seemed to diminish to nothing when the adults left the room. When it was only children about, he spoke clearly and without pause.

"I have a question?"

"What is your question, Little Alice?"

"Why must he sleep so? He seems to never wake, and even when I pet him, he only fidgets a little and goes back to sleep."

"That is because dormice hibernate this time of the year. He will probably sleep this way for months. I suggest putting more grass and leaves in there for him and maybe a few nuts if he gets hungry. Eventually, he will wake up and want to go back to a tree. You will need to let him go then, or else you will be a cruel lady indeed. Promise me you will let him go when it is time."

"I promise."

He stood to make his way to my father's study, but he turned to look back at me before he left me all alone.

"I will see you again, Miss Alice. Perhaps, to photograph you."

Thus began our adventures in wonderland together.

Chapter Two

Such an odd fellow was this Mr. Dodgson, but I too was the odd sort. I had once heard a friend of my mother's, a relatively plain and simple woman, remark at the unnerving depth in my eyes.

"She seems more aware than most children, does she not?"

My mother smiled at me the way she always did when adults spoke of her children without acknowledging their presence in a room. For all her faults, my mother was a woman who was just as aware as I was, and I had inherited my eyes from her.

"Alice is keenly aware of her presence in the world, Mrs. Greaves. Even if you are not."

I remember trying not to laugh at the joke, and Mrs. Greaves looked moderately offended. Her visits diminished after that encounter, but Mother did not seem to mind.

Therefore, when Mr. Dodgson, in all his odd ways,

made his appearance in our lives, I was powerless against him. Grown people rarely regarded children, let alone spoke to them as though they were capable of conversation, but not Mr. Dodgson. He spoke often about the folly of dismissing children. He'd visit us in the garden behind our home when Pricks allowed us time outside, and we'd have lovely discussions about all sorts of things.

The first things I remember about the gentleman was that he adored games. Chess and croquet were among his favorites. He even invented games himself for all of us to play, going so far as to fashion game pieces and puzzles from wire and wood. The man always had small books of silly poetry and games with him. It was like having regular visits from Father Christmas. His books were fun, unlike the others for children at the time. There were no morals or lessons in them, only nonsense.

We joked that the first thing Pricks noticed about the man was his face and manner. Mr. Dodgson was a handsome man, as far as Ina explained handsome to me. She had said Mr. Dodgson was handsome because he wore his hair longer than was the style, and his face was asymmetrical. For some reason, that made him handsome.

Pretty was a far easier concept to grasp as a young girl. Girls were pretty. Even ugly little girls were pretty. Most ladies were pretty until they turned cross, and then, they really were not pretty anymore. Mother was pretty all the time. Yet handsome, it was an idea that was hard for me to pinpoint. To think of my brothers or my father as handsome seemed awkward and ridiculous.

Pricks seemed to think Mr. Dodgson was handsome. She laughed too hard at even his silliest rhymes and smiled like a crocodile whenever he looked her way. He never seemed to acknowledge her strange manner and chose instead to concentrate on whatever game we were playing. Rumor fluttered about the house for a time that Mr. Dodgson used us children as a way to court Pricks, but he dismissed this as ridiculous. He treated the rumors as though they were so below him, he needn't acknowledge their existence at all. I liked him even more for this and dubbed him handsome indeed.

Harry grew tired of playing with us, citing our silly, girlish games as the reason. It was a warm afternoon in the garden when Harry said as much and stomped off to find other companions with better games and conversation. Mother called after him about rudeness, but he did not respond. To my surprise, Mr. Dodgson did not care.

"Boys may go as they like and play. Give me girls as friends any day."

"You do not like boys?" I asked.

"They are fine when they are younger, but all too soon they grow up and bully. Girls are far more interesting company, don't you agree?"

"Of course," I said thinking of Harry and his recent tendency to pull my hair and squeal like a pig when I walked by.

"Let us not discuss such trivial things as boys and brothers when there is a game to enjoy."

We were playing at cards, and I was winning. I smiled at the delightfully strange man while Ina, exasperated with math, sighed dramatically into the open pages of her book. She was three years my senior and struggling with her math workbook.

"Such things as these figures are truly not worth my time. They make no sense at all," lamented Ina.

Pricks passed by with a strict look.

"You must do them, Lorina. I will help if you need, but you should learn them without help. The figures stick better if you think them up yourself."

"Who would want to? Who would wish to sit about all day and work math?"

Mother and Pricks sat upright then and regarded Mr. Dodgson with curious stares. A laugh was hiding just below Mother's lips.

"Why Ina, Mr. Dodgson is a math lecturer here at Christ Church. Didn't you know?"

In that moment I wished Harry had stayed, for poor Ina's face was that of horror too funny to be reproduced. No amount of effort on my part mimicking the scene later could ever match it.

"Oh Mr. Dodgson, I am so very sorry."

Mother and Pricks laughed, and I joined in as quietly as I could. I hated when people laughed at me, so I tried to hide my indulgence. Regardless, Ina's face flushed red as a strawberry.

Mr. Dodgson smiled sympathetically but did not laugh. Mother and Pricks rose and left us there to prepare the afternoon tea, still laughing at Ina's folly. As soon as they left, Mr. Dodgson recited a poem for us with a silly look on his face.

"Multiplication can be a vexation,

Division is just as bad.

The rule of three doth puzzle me,

And practice drives me mad."

We laughed and Ina relaxed. In the spirit of the mood, I jumped up and ran to her.

"Let me see the book."

She opened the pages wider and showed me the interior of the beast. It was all so confusing. The numbers and symbols and such made no sense to me. It was from the lesson books above me, and there were no pictures to help at all.

"No pictures? How is one supposed to read a book with no pictures or funny conversation?"

Mr. Dodsgon rose from our abandoned game and joined us.

"I shall help you," he said simply.

I saw the relieved look on poor Ina's face. She smiled at him with all the care of a lady welcoming home her shining knight in armor. He was a hero, the handsome sort of hero, and Ina gazed at him while he dryly explained the math in front of her as though he were reading her poetry.

"Perhaps I should ask Father to let me attend one of your lectures, Mr. Dodgson," she said admiringly.

"Oh my dear Ina, I hate to see a young lady cry, and if you should attend my lecture, it shall bore you to tears."

She smiled even wider, and we all laughed.

As a child, I did not see the moment for what it was or for what it later would mean. Had I known, things might have been different.

Chapter Three

I mentioned that I had first seen Mr. Dodgson in front of the cathedral photographing someone. He was actually quite known for his love of photography, and his favorite subjects were children. It was only a matter of time before he had invited us to his apartment on campus to photograph me, Ina, and Edith. We loved these adventures. Photography was such a novelty to us, and Mr. Dodgson made the whole experience such fun.

An avid lover of the theater, Mr. Dodgson costumed us in various ways. We would act out great tales from the bible or even stories of chivalry and royalty. He always did find the idea of kings and queens entertaining.

One time, the three of us were princesses, posed with Ina in the center, since she was by far the tallest. Little Edith was having a difficult time sitting still as needed. She kept slumping with the little crown Mr. Dodgson had fashioned for her falling down below her eyes. Mother chided her to obey.

"Now Edith dear, you must sit up properly and be still.

Mr. Dodgson requires you to be like a statue."

"Mrs. Liddell, if I may. P-p-perhaps you might join the girls? A lovely queen with her p-princesses?"

I did so want Mother to leave. Mr. Dodgson was so much more relaxed when the adults were away. We could play unheeded and without all that silly stammering.

Mother's face was only visible to me for an instant, but I saw the shock on it. It was a look of indignant shock as she turned to Mr. Dodgson. So sudden was it that my mouth fell open. I knew that look and wanted to warn the man, but alas, she spoke before I could.

"That is not a possibility, and I'll thank you to not speak to me in that manner," she said sharply.

Poor Mr. Dodgson's lip quivered a little and he stood as still as a board. What relaxation he could find with Mother here was gone, replaced with extreme tension.

"I-I-I apologize."

"You should. To think of a married woman posing in a children's picture."

"I-I d-d-did not mean to offend — "

"Well, you did."

Mother turned to Edith suddenly.

"Edith, sit up straight now."

Little Edith did as she was told, and Mr. Dodgson took the photograph. In a short and hurried tone, Mother bade us to remove our costumes and ready for home. We did as we were told. When children sense an adult quarrel, their natural reaction is swift obedience, lest one find oneself in the middle.

Mr. Dodgson was putting away his things and working up some courage at the same time. By the time we were dressed, he had softened his face and relaxed his shoulders enough to talk to Mother.

He took her hand gently which was the worst thing he could possibly do.

"Mrs. Liddell, I—"

"Release my hand, sir."

He did so and stumbled over his words again. "I-I-I meant to compliment, n-not offend."

"Compliments are for my husband to pay me."

He bowed his head. "Yes, of course."

She grabbed Ina's hand who held Edith's who held mine. In tandem, we left his apartment, me looking back at him imploringly. He only gazed back in a sad way as we left him. Mother was so incensed that we were not allowed to visit with him for a good while. No more fun games, no more photographs, and no more curious Mr. Dodgson.

Her manner softened with some time and the constant begging of her three daughters. Yet, even when she and Father were to go on holiday together, she forbade us from visiting the man. I wondered what he had done that was so terrible. A compliment surely was not grounds for banishment.

Ina and I often played spies and snuck down to the

parlor at night when we knew our parents were discussing the details of the day. The night before their departure, we did that very thing in order to spy on their conversation. There was a table near the door that hid us well but allowed us to watch them undetected. We had done so before without anything interesting to show for it, but this time was different. They were discussing the matter of Mr. Dodgson just as we made it to our post.

"What is your issue with him?" asked Father.

"He was just too...familiar."

"He said you were pretty."

"The word he used was lovely, and it's inappropriate."

"Oh Lorina, really. Has no one ever called you lovely?"

"No one other than you!"

"I think you are being too hard on the man. Dodgson is an odd fellow, but a good one. He has such a charitable nature about him."

"And the rumors about him using the girls to court the governess?"

"You really listen to senseless servant rumors? Even Charles balked at the idea of courting a governess. I've seen the man here. He doesn't pay that woman any more attention than you do."

Mother and Father paced to a part of the room blocked by the frame of the door. There was a silence between them, and I wished we could peek around the corner to see what they were doing. That would give us away, of course.

"The girls do love him, and he does go through a lot of trouble to make them happy," she said.

"And he wrote you several letters of apology."

"Yes."

"Then, chalk the matter up to a slip of the tongue, and stop torturing us all. I'm tired of hearing the girls complain all the time."

It was silent, but I could almost imagine Mother's face. It was that pained expression she got when she lost an argument. We did not see it often, but if anyone could bring it out in her, it was Father.

Ina and I smiled at one another before sneaking back to our rooms. The next day the verbal ban of Mr. Dodgson still held, but we saw her tell Pricks that it was all right if he visited while they were away.

Chapter Four

Time softened Mother to Mr. Dodgson the way it does to people, and we all became fast friends again. When I was six, she commissioned him to do a portrait of me dressed as a beggar girl. This was my favorite portrait he did. We kept a hand-painted version of it in a lovely leather-bound frame in our parlor. Visitors always remarked on it, and Mr. Dodgson received many more eager parent patrons through us.

As my mother's temper eased, it also removed the more formal nature of our time together. Mr. Dodgson stammered so horribly when introducing himself to people, that the "Dodgson" part often ended up being "Do-do-Dodgson." Rather than shrink from these moments of embarrassment, he would use it as a game, calling himself a Dodo. He even took Ina, Edith, and I to the part of the Oxford Library where there was a skeleton of the infamous bird on display under glass. It was held together with wire and twine, but you could imagine what an awkward sort of animal that skeleton would make.

I pictured it bumbling about the sand of a beach the way Mr. Dodgson bumbled about his words when around people other than us and dubbed it a fine comparison. He became "Dodo" to me or "my Dodo" or "Uncle Dodo." Of course, Ina never call him that. She was more proper than I, but Edith readily adopted the name.

Every day with Dodo was an adventure in nonsense. He told us silly rhymes, wrote funny letters, and recited stories filled with utter absurdity. He would invent games off the cuff as if it was nothing for him to conjure things out of thin air. Dodo could write in mirror image just as easily as he could normally, and he'd write notes for us to run inside and translate in the sitting room mirror. We knew no one like him, and to us, he was a magician who wove our long, tedious days in pure, golden silk. I never noticed a thing out of place, not a hint of what was to come, until the year I turned eight and Ina was eleven.

Ina was lovely. Even as a child, her beauty was not small and childlike as might be fitting a young girl. She was tall and slender like a woman by the time she came running into my room screaming, blood staining her fingers. Her face was a colorless sort, and I thought she might faint right there.

"Alice, I'm bleeding!"

"From where? What happened?"

She made as though she wanted to tell me, but the horror killed the words before she formed them. I started looking over her body for a wound as Ina covered her mouth with her unsullied hand. For the life of me, I could see nothing amiss about her. No wound was visible.

"Where are you hurt? I do not see anything."

Ina just shook her head with a blank look, as though she were suddenly simple. I wanted to slap her, thinking perhaps she had gone silent with hysterics and needed a slap, but Mother walked in before I could manage it.

"Ina, what is the matter?"

Mother looked at the expression on her face and at the bloodied fingers by her side. Her face turned suddenly soft with an understanding I couldn't see.

"Dear, did this happen in the washroom?"

Ina nodded but said nothing.

"All right, come with me. We need to discuss something."

"Mother, is she all right?" I asked, confused.

"She will be fine, Alice."

"Why is she bleeding?"

"It is something that happens. You will learn about in it your own time. Now, I must take Ina away and clean her up. Go play with Edith."

Mother whisked Ina away, and I was left alone. It was a rainy day, so playing in the garden was out of the question, and no one of interest visited. Even Pricks had the day off, and for once, I longed for her company. Any company would do. Edith was fun for a while, but her childishness quickly grew tiresome.

Ina did not come down for the rest of the day. She sulked and haunted the upper rooms like a phantasm. When I tried to convince her to come down, she angrily yelled at me to leave her be. Everything was strange and different all of the sudden, and no one would tell me why.

The next morning began as usual. I rose with Edith and ate breakfast with Mother and Pricks. Ina finally joined us, but her face was raw from crying. She would not look at any of us, at least not for long. When I tried to meet her eyes, she turned away and glared down at her shoes.

Father joined us in his hurried fashion. He had a round belly that was always buttoned neatly under his waistcoat. He flitted about the room in a great hurry, as he was late again. Father was most often late.

"Dear, perhaps some breakfast?" coaxed Mother.

"No time, my dear. I'm terribly late," he said pulling his watch from his waistcoat and shaking his headed. "Late, so very late."

He muttered to himself and left us then. Father was never around for breakfast.

When Dodo arrived, I thought my heart might fly right out of my chest, a phrase he would have scolded me for had I said it aloud. For all his nonsense, he detested silly phrases that were used too often. I once dubbed a plate "broken into a thousand pieces", and he quickly explained how impossible that was.

He smiled when Edith and I ran to him, kisses ready for his cheeks. However, even Dodo's arrival could not seem to break Ina's sour mood. In fact, it only seemed to cause her more discomfort. Instead of playing in the parlor with us and our two new kittens, Dinah and Villikins, Ina stayed sullenly in the corner in an armchair with a book. Her posture was stiff, and she nearly jumped like a frightened bird any time Dodo tried to speak with her.

Dodo gave up trying to include her, and instead concentrated on the tabbies tussling about before us. Before long, we were all singing.

"As Villikins was a-val-i-king in his garden one day,

He called his dear Dinah and to her did say:

Go dress yourself Dinah in gorg-e-ous array,

And I'll bring you a hus-i-band both lov-er-ly and gay!

Singing tooral-i-tooral-i-ay."

All sang except Ina, who buried her nose further in her book. Our merriment was infectious, yet she seemed immune in her bubble of woe.

"Did you know," began our Dodo, "that ancient Egyptians worshipped cat as gods?"

"They did?" asked Edith.

"In fact, they did. They even made mummies of some, like they were pharaohs."

Edith and I gawked at him, unbelieving. We knew of mummies. Such tales of Egyptian treasures and mummies were all the rage in England at the time, but the idea of a cat mummy seemed unbelievable.

"That is a lot of nonsense," said Ina sullenly from the

chair.

The sudden need to defend his tale consumed me, and I glared at the book hiding Ina's melancholy visage. Her sullen mood had become far too irksome to tolerate.

"I'm sure Uncle Dodo would not lie," I said.

"He lies all the time. That is what he does. All those silly stories."

"Now Ina, I tell stories to amuse, but they are not lies. They are fiction. But this is truth I tell you about the mummies. Nothing fanciful here. They found a cache of cat mummies buried in Egypt, so many in fact, they did not know what to do with them all."

He was speaking directly to me now, and I was completely at his mercy. Those words wrapped around me like a warm blanket. I had missed them so. Edith listened from the fireplace, still playing with Dinah and Villikins.

"In fact, there were so many that they sold thousands of them to a company here who ground up the mummies and sold them as fertilizer to farmers."

"They did what? How is that possible?"

"It is true."

"Did they sell it to farmers where you are from, in Cheshire?" I asked excitedly.

"Indeed they did. That is how I know of it, and it is why our cats are so famous."

Edith put down the kitten and scooted her way closer to us. I was on my knees now, completely enraptured by his tale. Ina shifted in her chair, watching from the corner of her eye. Dodo smiled the way he did when he recognized how captive his audience had become.

"You see, my little birds, cats in Cheshire are always smiling. No matter what happens, they are the happiest cats in the world."

"Why?" asked Edith, hugging Dinah to her.

"Because they know the secrets of life. They smile the sly smile of an animal who knows something sacred, something no one else knows. When the Egyptian cat mummies were ground up and spread along the land, their spirits haunted everything they touched. Thus, the cats and kittens that lived on the land came face to face with their divine ancestors, who told them the secret of life."

We inched closer and closer to him, suspense stiffening out limbs.

"What is the secret of life?" I asked.

"I have no idea," remarked Dodo with a smile. "I'm not a cat, and they refuse to tell me."

"Oh you!"

I stood and mock slapped his cheek. He laughed and smiled wider.

"I am terribly sorry, young Miss Alice, but I am afraid the cats of Cheshire are the only ones who know such things. Perhaps someday you should visit and ask one yourself."

We laughed and laughed, all except Ina, who sat miserably by herself.

"Rubbish," she muttered into her book.

"What was that, dear Ina?" asked Dodo.

"It's a lot of rubbish," she said suddenly standing, her book falling to the floor.

The merriment was gone in an instant.

"This is all far too ridiculous for one to take. All of it. It is a lot of nonsense."

"Ina, stop being so nasty. He's just trying to tell us a story," I said, scowling at her.

She had been glaring at Dodo, but when she turned her venom on me, she could have burned holes through my skull.

"You would protect him, your precious Dodo. You are, after all, his favorite. You've always been his favorite. It's as plain as day who he loves most."

She was angry, but tears began to show themselves at the edge of her eyes. Edith, hating fights in general, slunk away and hid behind a table with the kittens while I stared down Ina without knowing what to say.

"Ina, what a terrible thing to say. I love you equally," chastised Dodo in his Uncle voice.

"That is a lie," she spat at him. "You love her the most, you always have. You take more pictures of her, you dote on her, and you tell her all the best stories."

Dodo stood then and tried to walk to her, nothing but

comfort in his face. Ina refused to give him the chance. She pushed him away and ran from the room sobbing. When he turned back around to face me, I saw it in his eyes. There was exasperation surely, perhaps even a tinge of regret, but beyond all that, in a space only I could read, I saw that what Ina said was true. I was his favorite.

Chapter Five

Ina would not discuss the matter with me, nor would she accompany me to Dodo's house for weeks. With extreme disappointment, I decided to shake myself of her and her blathering. Jealousy was a terrible bedfellow, and he had seemed to take up residence in Ina's sullen room. Therefore, Edith and I saw my Dodo alone, at least without Ina, for a time.

I have not spoken of his apartment yet, save for the fact it doubled as a photography studio. However, the place was a wonder for any child to see. We would follow Dodo through the quadrangle and past Tom's Tower, all particularly lovely in the springtime, to spend an afternoon playing in his apartment.

The magic of that place was beyond measure for me. Such a creative man was he that there were little wooden puzzles he fashioned just for small hands to play with. There were mind teasers made of wire and string. One particular afternoon, I noticed there was an odd creature made of fabric and wood and painted green. It was a new addition, and I asked about it.

"Oh that. That was a thing inspired by our talk last Wednesday, dear Alice. We were dining on mock turtle soup at your home, and you asked me what a mock turtle looked like. I decided to make one for you."

I looked at the thing. So queer was the creature, I began to giggle.

"Why, it looks like a calf on a turtle's body. And the ears, they are like a hare's."

Edith sauntered over and took the toy down to better inspect the creature. She giggled along with me.

"It looks mad as a March Hare, Uncle," she said with great enthusiasm.

She ran away from us, hugging it like a doll. Dodo laughed, but there was something behind his eyes. When you really know a person, you can see behind the eyes they show to everyone else. There is a space, however small, that provides a window to their mind. The tiny space behind Dodo's eyes spoke of stress not discussed.

"What's wrong, Uncle Dodo?"

He gazed at me for a moment, seeing my own space, I supposed.

"How do you know there is something wrong?"

I gave him a level look. He laughed a little but not because I was funny.

"You resemble your mother when you look at me like that. She's a no-nonsense woman, something I admire about her. I suppose you are a no-nonsense girl?"

"I like nonsense when it's fashioned in one of your stories."

"Yes, but in life, you are very much like her."

He looked at me then in a way I did not understand. The space beneath his eyes told things I did not understand.

"What is it?" I asked.

"Oh, life can be petty sometimes. That is why I love seeing you children. You relax me. It is like being home again. In Cheshire, I had many brothers and sisters, and I made them things like these. It was the happiest I ever was."

"So, why are you so tense now? Is it because of Ina?"

"Ina? No, certainly not. Ina is just changing as all girls must. She might be too old to enjoy her old Uncle anymore. These things happen."

"I think she may be in love with you," I blurted without thinking.

I surprised him, but I was quite possibly even more surprised. The thing I had spoken was a secret, and not one I even thought I knew. Yet, as soon I said it, I somehow was sure it was true.

"I am sure if it is anything, it is just a schoolgirl's fancy. Ina is a lovely girl, and she will find boys her own age appealing soon enough."

There was something in my heart, or perhaps it sat just

above my heart in an empty part of my ribcage, that told me otherwise. I kept my mouth shut on the topic as it seemed to make him uncomfortable.

"And what about you? What sort of girls did you fancy as a boy? Edith and I were hoping you might marry soon so we might be flower girls in your wedding."

He tensed again. I was not sure what I had said, but it was a wrong thing.

"I did fancy a girl once...before I came to Oxford. She was so lovely, but..."

Dodo never intended to tell me the memory behind it. With a quick shake, he shut the door to the tiny space in his eyes, and a happy mask replaced it.

"Enough past and gloom. Today is my unbirthday, did you know?"

"Your unbirthday? What do you mean?"

"Well, everyone has a birthday, but did you know that you have three hundred and sixty four unbirthdays in a year? That is a number that argues how far better unbirthdays are, I do think."

I grinned widely at him, picking up on the game.

"Sweet Uncle, then it is *my* unbirthday too," I said.

"Then, you must join the dance, fair Alice. Will you won't you will you won't you please join the dance?"

We laughed and danced around one another, he acting like I was royalty and bowing to me as I curtsied. Edith ceased her playing with the mock turtle and came over to see the fuss.

"What's going on?"

"Oh dear Edith, today is mine and Dodo's unbirthday!" She smiled.

"Your unbirthday?"

"Yes, dear Edith. My word, I believe it is your unbirthday too!"

"It is?"

"Yes, and you must join our dance!" I screamed pulling her alongside me.

Edith always was such a happy girl, and she readily joined in the fun. We danced about and acted like royal clowns, the three of us.

"I believe this is an occasion for Bob the Bat," said Dodo proudly.

"Bob the Bat? Who might he be?"

"Oh, you will see."

Dodo danced to a cupboard and reached inside. He produced a rather terrifying thing. It was a bat fashioned by his own hand. It was made of wire and painted gauze with red buttons for eyes. The thing was frightening and captivating at the same. We stared at it in amazement.

"This is Bob, you see," said Uncle holding out the thing.

We nodded, not daring to touch him.

"And did you know that Bob can fly?"

"He can?" we asked in unison.

"He can, but let us sing his song, shall we? Twinkle little bat, how I wonder where you're at," said Dodo while winding a string and propeller around some gadget in the bat's body.

"Twinkle little bat, how I wonder where you're at," we repeated, watching the thing, both frightened and excited.

"And off he goes!"

Dodo shouted as he flung the creature into the air and his wings began flapping wildly. We screamed in delight as the bat flew in circles above our heads. The moment of flight was brief, and just as quickly ended as the bat made for the opened window and hurled itself into the great outside. We all ran to the window to watch its perilous flight downward from the second-floor apartment and straight toward a steward carrying a tray of salad and tea for some professor. Before we could utter a squeak of warning, the bat collided with the tray, spilling the salad and breaking a teacup.

We ducked underneath the window instinctively, not wanting to be caught, as the poor steward screamed. I had to press both hands over my face in order not to laugh loudly and give us away. Edith giggled uncontrollably, and Dodo did the same.

"Quick, Alice, do you think it is his unbirthday as well?" asked Dodo.

"Well, I'd say there is a good chance that it is. Three hundred and sixty four to one."

"Then, let us wish him a very merry unbirthday from

Bob the Bat."

We three stood then and stuck our heads out of the window. The steward looked at us with an astonished glare. His eyes were as wide as saucers.

"A very merry unbirthday to you!" we screamed in unison.

The steward looked rather cross, but we dropped back to the floor and laughed until our sides hurt. It was the best unbirthday I had ever had.

Chapter Six

To know the man called Charles Dodgson, you first would have to understand something about him that did not exactly fit with the whimsical fellow, Lewis Carroll. He was intensely devout, in fact a deacon at Christ's Church, as most professors were. His lectures were often dry and tedious to sit through, even considered so by other math enthusiasts. He stammered often and gave as few lectures as he could. Mr. Dodgson wrote mathematical textbooks, ones so dry and boring I could not read beyond a few pages before nodding off to sleep.

To have two such fellows living in one body must have been a strange affair indeed. The man who sang rhymes and built puzzles Saturday, was strict about respectfully attending services on Sunday. Dodo told us often how important the church was, yet he often told Mother that little children should not be expected to endure a Sunday service without something to entertain them. He often prescribed fun books or quiet puzzles to keep the younger ones happy and busy. Mother, like most parents, was confused by the idea.

"How might the children learn the word of God if they are busy with something else?"

"Young children's minds are n-not ready to understand such things," he remarked. "Let them see church as a quiet b-b-but fun place, a retreat if you will. As they grow, they p-p-put down childish things and learn."

Most were not convinced, but my mother was. We were allowed to bring picture books and puzzles to church, as long as we were respectfully silent, and Dodo was our savior for it. Ina, however, was not ready to participate. She had refused to accompany us on many of our outings with Dodo since her outburst. I could not decide if she was embarrassed or just hurt, but the rift vexed me. Ina was just being silly, and every time I tried to speak to her about the matter, she flushed red and left the room.

One Sunday, our family arrived at church to find Dodo waiting outside the main entrance. He looked handsome as always and smiled at us as we approached. Edith and I ran to him, arms outstretched. He was bombarded with little girl hugs and kisses. With a great smile he greeted Mother and Father and Ina. All smiled cheerfully at him, except Ina, who nodded politely but looked away.

"My dear Ina, I have a gift for you," said Dodo, reaching inside his coat with one gloved hand.

"I am a little old for picture books, Mr. Dodgson," she retorted.

Mother's faced dropped. "Ina, apologize this instant!

What sort of well-bred girl responds such as that? I am sorry dear Mr. Dodgson for my daughter's rudeness."

Dodo appeared as though he hadn't heard a word of Ina's scathing remarks. He produced a handwritten book bound in leather. Ina perked up a bit and took the gift from him gently.

"No apologies necessary. This is something special, Ina."

"What's that you have there, Dodgson?" asked Father.

"Well sir, you know how I was t-t-tinkering with the idea of making Shakespeare appropriate f-for younger ears? Well, this is my first attempt. I think it's rather good."

Ina opened it and there was the title written in amateur calligraphy.

Romeo and Juliet

"I thought Ina m-m-might enjoy it. If she approves, perhaps I'd d-d-do others."

Father laughed heartily and slapped Dodo on the back. Mother looked a little worried. Ina held the book to her chest and smiled at Mr. Dodson for the first time in months.

"But Mr. Dodgson, such a play. Would it not be inappropriate for Ina to read such a thing?" said Mother.

"No n-n-not at all. You see, I have simplified the

language and cut out certain...more adult parts."

"Yes, all the good bits. I'm surprised you didn't try to tackle Hamlet," said Father with a loud chuckle.

Dodo looked at him very seriously. "Oh sir, t-t-to make Hamlet for children, I fear there may not be enough left to fill two pages."

Father laughed harder despite, or perhaps because of, Dodo's blank face. "Probably just be the ghost left. There's always a ghost, is there not?"

A round of laughter sounded from the adults, even Dodo.

I thought hard for a moment before chiming in. "Yes, but also Rosencrantz and Guildenstern. They would be appropriate."

Everyone stopped their conversation and turned to look at me. Father ceased his laughing, and by the look on their faces, I had a suspicious feeling that I had done something wrong. Only Dodo smiled now in that way he did when I managed to surprise him in a favorable manner.

"You have read Hamlet, Alice?" asked Mother.

I did not know what to say. Something like a little lizard crawling around in my head told me to lie and lie quickly. However, that smile on Dodo's face was reassuring enough that the truth spilled forth instead.

"Yes. It was in Father's library. Was I not supposed to?"

Just then, the bells gonged, announcing the beginning of the Sunday services. I had never been so thankful for their loud pronouncements. The focus moved away from me and on to bustling our way into the church. Ina sat next to me as usual, clutching the little book Dodo had given her to her chest. I hadn't seen her so happy in ages. She slept with the thing in her bed and read it over and over again until the pages began to fray.

Eventually, she agreed to let me read it. Truly, I did not know what all the fuss was about. To me, it was a boring read compared to its original. Dodo had cut out all the jokes and the best parts.

Chapter Seven

There was a day, like any other day at the time, but a day nonetheless that would prove to be one of those historical markers in the world. For those present, we found it funny not to recognize it as such. Perhaps most people live memorable days without ever knowing their significance except through the clear lens of retrospect. The facts of the day vary based on who tells this tale as well. Ina would swear the day was chilly and a bit wet, while Dodo and I swear that it was clear and warm. Edith remembers the weather as too hot indeed. For the sake of sanity, I will tell of the day as I remembered it.

It was a clear and warm afternoon on July 4th of 1862 when Edith, Ina, and I accompanied Uncle Dodo and his friend, Reverend Robinson Duckworth, for an outing. We were going to go row along the Thames. I was ten then and Ina was thirteen. Mother had started to become more insistent that Ina have chaperones during our outings with Dodo, not because she didn't trust our dear Uncle but because Ina was now considered old enough to entertain suitors. People might start rumors if a girl Ina's age were out alone in the company of a bachelor, hence the added company of Reverend Duckworth. None of us minded, of course. He was an excellent rower and friend of Uncle Dodo's. Edith dubbed him "completely pleasant in every way."

We began our great voyage at Folly Bridge, near Oxford, with the intention of reaching the village of Godstow before stopping for tea. The day was mild, clear and thankfully devoid of other boats on the water. When I looked over the edge, the water was like glass reflecting perfect mirrors images of us all. Dodo, Ina, Edith, Reverend Duckworth, and I stared back up at me from the glassy reflection. Only the occasional ripple marred the likeness. The fun of the journey began as most did, with we three girls begging Uncle for a story.

"Oh please, Mr. Dodgson," pleaded Ina.

"You must tell us a story," said Edith.

Dodo smiled over his shoulder and agreed to our demands as he always did.

"And make sure there is a good deal of nonsense!" I chimed.

Everyone laughed, and then Uncle began.

"All in the golden afternoon

Full leisurely we glide;

For both our oars, with little skill,

By little arms are plied,

While little hands make vain pretense

Our wanderings to guide."

Reverend Duckworth looked curiously at his friend over his right shoulder. If it had been the reflection version of himself, it would have been his left. The ease at which Dodo's rhymes came to him seemed to perplex the young scholar.

"Is this something prepared, Charles?"

"No, flying from the cuff, I'm afraid," replied Dodo with a smile.

"Impressive. I have no mind for rhymes."

"Nonsense and rhymes, my fellow, are all that keep me sane."

"Oh, do go on," pleaded Ina.

We all repeated her pleas over and again until he continued with his story.

"Imperious Prima flashes forth

Her edict to 'begin it' —

In gentler tones Secunda hopes

'There will be nonsense in it' —

While Tertia interrupts the tale

Not more than once a minute."

We giggled knowing each our name and part for it was true that Edith loved to interrupt again and again. Ina was Prima, I was Secunda, and Edith was Tertia. He then wove a lovely tale of a world never dared imagined, of Hatters quite mad, tears that could flood, and a shrinking girl named Alice. Yes, I was the main character, but Ina and Edith were there too. Ina was a Lory in a great caucus race with an Eaglet, and a Duck, among other things. Reverend Duckworth was the Duck and Edith was the Eaglet. Uncle had portrayed himself too as the Dodo, and we all laughed at our parts.

So much lovely nonsense, yet there were parts of our lives at every corner. The mock turtle, the unbirthday party, and even the cards were reminiscent of our long afternoons with our favorite Uncle. One of my favorite parts was of a Cheshire cat who smiled endlessly and disappeared on a whim. We had tea on a lovely hill near town where the story continued. It went on and on, and none of us wished it to end.

He teased us mercilessly. Alice would just be about to begin another adventure, and Dodo would feign nodding off for a nap right there in the middle of the story! We would jump up and scream at him to continue, even going so far as to bribe him with kisses. With a start, he'd pretend to wake and continue.

There were rhymes we knew, every child knew them, but in this new world Dodo described, they were different and so much more entertaining. There were no lessons or morals to learn. It was all just great fun. "How doth the little busy bee, improve each shining hour," became "How doth the little crocodile, improve his shiny tail."

The funniest part was when the red queen of hearts

shouted, "Off with their heads!" Such a scene was silly enough, but Dodo did her voice in the same way he mimicked Pricks for us when she wasn't present. I pictured Pricks in the finery of royalty, shouting until red in the face. I rolled on the grass and clutched my sides from laughter.

It was a quarter past eight before we managed to return to Christ Church. Dodo led us all to his apartment to show us some new photographs. Even though the day had been lovely, like most days with Dodo, something about the story he spun for us stuck inside my mind, unwilling to leave me alone. After walking us home, he went to kiss my cheek goodbye, but I moved so that he missed his mark.

"Is there something the matter, Alice?"

"No Uncle, I just wanted to ask you a favor."

"What is it?"

"Will you write that down for me?"

"Write what down?"

"The story with the Hatter, and the Dodo, and the Queen. The story about me and the Cheshire cat. Will you write it down for me? Please?"

He smiled and kissed my cheek. I did not move this time.

"Of course, my dear Alice. I promise I will."

Chapter Eight

It was later that year that we came to meet Lord Viscount Newry. He was eighteen and an undergraduate at Christ Church. Since he was from such a prestigious family, Mother invited him over for dinner several times. She smiled larger around him and acted extra gracious. The way she always sat him next to Ina told me her intensions. Mother was hoping to match the two in marriage. Ina seemed not to notice him most of the time. She was kind and polite, but preoccupied with something no one else could see, as was often her state of mind.

He was a handsome fellow, I suppose, but I did not like him right off. In fact, I never really liked the man at all. To say a specific reason would be beyond my capabilities, I'm afraid. There truly was no reason I should have disliked the fellow. He never was anything but gracious to me. However, one does not need a specific reason be wary of a serpent, does one? I no more wanted to shake his hand than I would pet a snake.

I remember thinking as much one evening when we

were entertaining Lord Newry and Dodo. The youngest children were sent to bed shortly after dinner, but Ina and I were allowed to stay for a while longer. The young lord did seem to find Ina beautiful. He said as much to her respectfully during dessert, but she only blushed and looked away.

Afterwards, it was customary for the gentlemen to retire to Father's study and talk among the fumes of cigars and brandy. The ladies would converse in the parlor. I was no lady and wanted none of Mother and Ina's conversation. This would normally be when Dodo and I would find a quiet corner to play a game or invent some new rhymes, but Lord Newry had his hand firmly on Uncle's back, leading him away from me. The look on my dear Dodo's face spoke volumes to me. He hated boring adult conversation as much as I did.

I decided then and there I wouldn't leave my friend to be bored to death by Father and the serpent, Lord Newry. There was no possible way to convince them to let me join, but I could sneak into the adjoining washroom and spy on them, waiting for an opportune moment to pull my Dodo away to freedom with me.

A few excuses about being tired pardoned me from the ladies' parlor, and I made my way to my Father's washroom. No one saw me, but the idea they could delighted and thrilled my imagination. When the men entered the room, I thought I might burst from excitement. Luckily, their conversation was so terribly dull that the extra energy leaked out of me within minutes. Father offered both men brandy and cigars. Dodo refused both politely. He looked uncomfortable all over, so I waited for my opportunity. I had lifted my favorite deck of cards from the parlor and hid it in my pockets. Now, I fingered the case tucked neatly away, itching to play with them to pass the time.

Conversation should be fun, or at the very least interesting. Father and Lord Newry found their conversation intensely interesting. Dodo and I did not.

"Tell me, Charles, may I call you Charles?" asked Lord Newry.

"Yes, Charles would b-b-b-be fine," stammered Dodo.

Lord Newry chuckled and slapped him on the back. "Quite the stammer you've got there, Charles. Must make your lectures a good deal longer, doesn't it?"

He laughed at his own joke, and Father smiled politely. My Uncle, my dear sweet Dodo, straightened his face and tried to keep his lip from trembling. I could see the extra effort, just like I could see the slight flush in his cheeks that he got when embarrassed. These men did not know him well enough to notice those things, nor did they see that the tight smile he grew was a difficult one for him to hold.

I hated Lord Newry. He was no longer Lord Newry. He was the Serpent Newry, perhaps even just the Serpent.

"Oh, you should tell Charles here about your plans for a ball," said Father, trying to change the subject.

"Ball?" asked Dodo.

"Yes, I was wanting to host a ball, right here at Christ Church," said the Serpent.

"B-b-but such things are not p-p-p-permitted."

"Look at this. We need more brandy," said Father with a smile.

He exited the room, leaving the Serpent there alone with my Dodo. I wanted to run out from hiding, kick the Serpent, and drag Uncle away. I did not do it. To give up my cover would give up the game, and I wanted to hear more about this ball.

"See here, Charles," began the Serpent in a conspiratorial tone. "I know the rules against balls here at Christ Church, but there is precedent for that rule to be overturned on a case by case basis. The faculty votes on the matter, and the majority rules. I've already got Dean Liddell on my side."

"You d-d-d-do?"

"Why yes, Mrs. Liddell as well. She's very keen on Alice and Ina being able to attend a ball here."

"Is she now?"

"Surely you've seen how she parades Ina in front of me? Just between the two of us, I could never marry a *dean's* daughter, but the girl is pretty. There are all sorts of fun to be had in the garden with girls like that. I'm sure you know all too well what I mean."

I had to cover my mouth to stifle the gasp that threatened to escape it. Uncle's face turned hard and red. It was rage, very well-managed rage, but intense nonetheless. The Serpent took it for embarrassment.

"No need to hold anything back from me," he said in a friendly way. "I'm sure you've taken your fair share of liberties. I know I'll have your backing when the vote comes to pass. We could have a lot of fun, you and I."

Dodo's hands were twitching a little at his side. I thought for a moment he might slap the young lord, but at the center of his heart stood a gentleman built from stone. He restrained himself with much difficulty before he spoke.

"Ina is only thirteen and a dear girl. Any liberties you had in mind should be removed immediately. You do *not* have my backing on this. You are lucky that I do not go directly to the dean with what you have just told me."

Uncle's blue eyes pierced the young Serpent's and left the lad stunned, mouth agape like a fish at the market. I smiled with the triumph of it.

"Your stammer, it is gone," said the Serpent, clearly in another world.

"That is not the only thing gone. If you come to this house again or call upon any of Mrs. Liddell's daughters, I will tell Dean Liddell what you have told me tonight. Then, you will be expelled, I guarantee it. Do you understand me?"

Still stunned, the Serpent nodded.

"The only reason I do not go to him this instant and ruin your reputation is that you are a young man, and young men make mistakes. You will not make such a foolish mistake again, will you?"

The Serpent Newry stared blankly.

"Will you?"

"No, I will not."

"Good. Tell Dean Liddell I felt ill. I'm leaving."

At that, my Uncle, my Dodo, my Mr. Dodgson walked out of that room. He might have been wearing his normal gray-and-black gloves and tidy hat as before, but to me, he was transformed. His waistcoat replaced by a shining breastplate, his hat by a glistening helmet, and his gloves with gauntlets. He was a knight in armor, and I knew I could tell no one of what he'd done.

Chapter Nine

"It was you, wasn't it?" demanded Mother.

"I b-b-beg your p-pardon?"

I was downstairs hiding in our usual place behind the table whenever we chose to spy on adults in the parlor. Yes, you might think I was too old for such things. Ina agreed I was. She was much too refined for such childish games, but she did not know what I knew. If she had, she would have been hiding with me right then, acting like a foolish child.

Mother had invited Dodo to the house but not to play games with us. Edith had a fever, and Ina and I had our lessons. She had asked him here in order to confront him. The vote for Lord Newry's ball proposal had been cast, and it was a resounding disappointment for the ladies of Christ Church. The faculty voted against it.

"I heard you voted against Lord Newry's ball and that you persuaded others to do so as well. Do you deny it?"

Dodo removed his hat and fiddled with the brim in his

hands. "No, I d-d-do not. It is true."

Mother crossed her arms and screwed her face into that contorted fashion she managed when truly vexed. "Why may I ask? After all we've done for you."

"It is against the law here for undergraduates to hold b-b-balls."

"My husband ordained you a deacon just last year despite your refusal to join the priesthood, a highly unorthodox thing. Yet, you took that liberty."

"Yes, and it was kind of him."

"How is this different?"

Dodo looked around the room as if searching for something unseen. I could see his lips twitching ever so slightly. "There was not sufficient reason to allow such a b-ball at this time."

I wanted to scream, for him to scream. It was beyond me why he refused to tell Mother what a scoundrel the Serpent was.

"And what is your reason for not joining the priesthood like so many of your fellows?" she asked pointedly.

He stopped fiddling with his hat and looked at her directly in the eye. "I d-d-d-do not understand why you are angry with me," he said with all sincerity.

"I am merely pointing out this hypocrisy. You manage to obtain special privileges here at Christ Church, yet you actively fight against someone else throwing a ball. Tell me, did you not wish to be ordained because you want to marry?"

Dodo looked taken aback. I wanted desperately to run to him, to defend him.

"I haven't any plans as yet..."

"So if you are free to change rules for yourself, why not for Lord Newry? You must know how a ball such as this would help Ina's station. Knowing such things and our family as you do, I cannot understand, Mr. Dodgson, why you would block this event."

"Mrs. Liddell, I b-b-blocked this event for good reason."

"Why? What is the reason? You knew how important this was to me and to Ina."

"I d-d-do not believe it meant much t-t-to Ina at all. And I d-d-did it for her benefit."

Mother cocked her head to one side. A quizzical look covered her face. "Is it Ina, Mr. Dodgson? Surely you are not skirting priestly vows for Ina? Is this entire campaign against the good Lord Newry to—"

"Absolutely not," interrupted Uncle. "Mrs. Liddell, with all d-due respect, I love Ina as I love all your children, as their d-d-dear Uncle. Ina may have crossed the line into maturity, b-b-but she is still a sweet child to me."

The sincerity on his face was sharp and undeniable. Mother's ardor softened, her shoulders relaxed. It was like watching a mother cat lowering her hackles in front of a litter of fresh, new kittens.

"Then why, Mr. Dodgson?"

She moved a little closer to him, her face soft. Mother took his gloved hand in order to coax him to speak. He looked at their hands touching and then looked into her face. I suddenly felt a tinge of guilt seeing them this way. The moment felt intimate in a way I rarely saw in adults. It was not something I understood completely, but the air between them altered. It stirred and buzzed like bees. I wanted to run away.

"Mrs. Liddell, I cannot say for g-g-good reasons. Please, you have known me for years, and you have allowed me to be a p-p-part of your family. Trust me. You must keep Ina and Alice away from Lord Newry."

Mother opened her mouth to say something to him but closed it with a second thought. She nodded and dropped her hands. The intimate moment was gone. I breathed a sigh of relief when it was all over.

Chapter Ten

Time passed, and the Lord Newry business passed as well. Mother never invited the young man to the house again, and as far as my knowledge carried me, Father did not ask why. Such matters of balls and dinner guests were of no consequence to him. As long as Mother was happy, Father was happy, or so was his unspoken motto.

We visited Dodo as before, except Mother rarely bothered to insist on a chaperone as she had the year prior. My only conclusion was that something had renewed her trust in Dodo, or she saw how silly worrying about what others thought truly was. Society would gossip no matter what happened, so why bother fighting the tide? Dodo had little use for gossip, and neither did I.

In 1863, I was eleven. I was told I was pretty but not nearly as much so as Ina. Ah, poor dear Ina. She was lovely beyond her years, both tall and fair, but her thoughts were mottled with romance. Never had she been a great scholar, but I feared the love letters she wrote to no one in particular would overtake her mind. At the very least, I was sure it was overtaking her good sense.

Young men wished to call upon her, and she entertained as she was now fourteen and at an appropriate age to do so with a chaperone present. Ina was gracious and courteous as might be fitting for a dean's daughter, but after each suitor left, she'd close herself away in her room once again to write letter after letter to someone who did not exist. They were never addressed to any of the boys. They simply were addressed to a Mr. Nobody.

I asked her once who Mr. Nobody was, and she said he was nobody. A great bit of nonsense but still, an aggravating one. She would never tell me more.

It was in June when Dodo invited Edith and me over to organize a trip to Nuneham with him. Even though she wasn't intended to accompany us on the trip, Ina asked to escort us to Uncle's apartment. She often invited herself along or invited him to her functions. We agreed, and the three of us set off for our destination, hand in hand.

It was a merry gathering. We sang songs for him, and he laughed. None of us had any true talent with singing, but he applauded all the same. He showed us pamphlets a friend had sent him about happenings in Nuneham. Edith and I rejoiced in the fun we would have, and Ina lamented her absence.

At one point, Dodo left us alone in the apartment. He had earlier told us he saw a rather incredible caterpillar feasting on a fern growing just below his window. He wanted to show us the creature before it cocooned itself, so he made his way outside to bring it forth. Edith and I set to playing a game of chess while we waited.

It had been at least ten minutes before I realized that not only had he been gone a good long while, but Ina was missing as well. Something in the back of my mind tickled my neck, causing bumps to rise up the tiny hairs that rested there. Things were amiss.

I told Edith she should play for me, and I made my way out of the apartment and into the surrounding garden. The sun was just beginning to set, casting colors this way and that. Blue shadows spread their fingers across everything. In one of those shadows, I saw Dodo. He was backed against a wall, and Ina was kissing him on the mouth. This was not a good Uncle kiss, it was a lover's kiss.

My voice caught in my throat as I stared at them, unsure what I was seeing. Before I managed to collect it again, Dodo had grabbed Ina by the shoulders and pulled her away from him.

"Ina, what are you doing?" he asked a little breathlessly.

"What I've always wanted to do," she said as if in a dream.

Ina tried to move forward, perhaps to kiss once more, but he held her at arm's length by her shoulders.

"This is not proper," he said flushed.

"But it is. I am fourteen now, and—"

"Ina, this is not...we are not..."

"But, but I love you, and you love me," said Ina, her voice tinged with a droplet of desperation.

"I love you, Ina, but as an Uncle loves his dear, young friend."

"But, you gave me the book, Romeo and Juliet, and all those days we spent together. All the hugs and... I have to be something more to you than a friend. I just have to. I have to mean more to you than Alice!"

"Dear Ina, you are a lovely girl, but..."

"But you are in love with her!" shouted Ina.

She broke her shoulders free from him and stomped one foot on the ground, like a child with a tantrum. We watched as her face filled with redness. She trembled as though she were boiling inside.

"Keep your voice down, Ina."

"I will not!"

"Ina!" I exclaimed as I moved out of my own shadow and walked into theirs. "What have you done?"

Embarrassment flooded her face as relief flooded Dodo's. Fresh tears filled her eyes and ran down her cheeks. Ina looked at me as though she were terrified of me, as though I were a panther. I stood in front of her, feeling as if I was growing, or she shrinking under my gaze. She was discovered and her secret was out. Mr. Nobody had a name indeed.

"Alice, I—"

Before she could finish, Ina clasped her hands over her

face and ran from us. Sorrow and embarrassment colored her skin as her form vanished into the distance. Dodo and I were left alone, staring at one another without the words to express the chaos in our minds. We stood like that for some time before I broke the silence.

"Edith is still upstairs. We should return to her," I said with little emotion.

However stern my words, my face gave away the confusion behind them. His face, likewise, held a violent storm of thoughts in that little gap underneath his eyes. Dodo nodded to me all the same.

"Yes, quite right, Alice. Will Ina be all right getting home, do you think?"

"She knows the way," I replied.

I was vague, not a true answer at all really.

"True, but do we?"

A silenced passed between us like an unannounced visitor. In the interim, he reached for my hand and held it in his. I squeezed his hand, dry and warm as it was, while we stared into the space where Ina had just vanished.

Chapter Eleven

I knew when she refused to talk to anyone something was coming. Ina often went through periods of seclusion, and sometimes it meant mainly being silent toward me. She often accused me of being so like Mother she wanted to scream. This time, however, Ina would not speak to anyone. Even Edith got the cold shoulder. Poor Edith. She knew nothing of what had happened. I told no one of what I saw that evening outside Dodo's apartment, including her. This sudden exile from Ina's good graces made even less sense to her.

The rumors started as they so often did, in whispers inside the house. As a young child, I had a firm belief that every rumor began life as an errant ghost who haunted the minds of servant girls and cooks. It was often the servants who spread such things so it seemed natural to think it. The funny rumors about Dodo and Pricks so long ago felt like that, nothing but silly ghosts filling the heads of servants. I was soon to realize that people, not ghosts, were the makers of rumors.

The whispers started innocently enough, among stewards in the dining hall, or so I'm told. Then, they spread to the cooks, which spread to our cook. I overheard her one evening while she and Sarah, the kitchen maid, were cleaning up after dinner.

"Yes, I thought it might've been the governess too, but apparently not. Those rumors are old ones anyway. Apparently, he's been using his love of the Liddell children to court young Ina without a chaperone for years."

"What a fiend! He seemed like such a nice sort of chap too. I liked Mr. Dodgson."

"Goes to show you never know a man, even one who loves children so."

I spun on my heel and left before they saw me. Whispers had made their way to the house, but I hoped Mother would pay no mind to them. She often ignored servant gossip. This seemed to be the case for a few days. I kept my ears open but heard nothing more of the sordid tales in the house.

It was not until I was walking through the quadrangle one day that I spotted Ina deep in giddy conversation with a friend of hers named Sarah. They were positioned near a group of young, undergraduate students and talking loud enough for them to overhear with ease.

"You would not believe the love notes I receive," said Ina, batting her eyelashes. "And did I tell you about the kiss? He pulled me to him, just like in a play. I have known the man so I long, but he is so handsome..."

The students nearby were listening intently, waiting for the name of the mysterious suitor to be revealed. Perhaps they already knew the name and were just waiting for the confirmation. Either way, I was on top of the two girls within a blink of an eye. The voice that came from me was not mine own. It was like my mother was speaking through me.

"Lorina Liddell, stop lying this instant!"

Both girls jumped and the students dispersed promptly. I was still a head shorter than Ina, but I stared into her eyes as though she were a worm.

"Alice!" Ina squeaked.

Sarah made a mumbled excuse before she too left our company.

"It's *you* starting these horrible rumors," I accused, pointing a finger at her. "Why Ina? Why are you telling these lies about him?"

The initial shock of me was beginning to wear off, and Ina stood straighter with a defiant look.

"Stick to your own business and stay away from mine, Alice."

"It is my business when you are spreading lies about our Uncle."

"You would defend him. You always defend him."

"What are you talking about?"

She shook her head as if there was something I could

not understand.

"Someday, you will see."

Before I could respond, Ina stormed away from me. I turned and ran toward home in the most unladylike fashion I could manage. I had to get to Mother before the rumors did. In a way, it was a useless effort, but I had to try. I just had to try.

Chapter Twelve

"Alice, I need you to be honest," said Mother seriously.

"I am being honest. I saw them together. Ina kissed *him.* Uncle was a gentleman, I swear it. He stopped her."

"You can see how I am skeptical. I know Ina can be infatuated at times, but perhaps Mr. Dodgson coaxed her? Did you see him act as a suitor might toward her? Oh, how I wish I had insisted on a chaperone."

"No, he did not. It is Ina, Mother. She thinks..."

I stopped before uttering the words. They were absurd to even say. Mother's eyebrow raised at me, sensing my hesitance.

"She thinks what, Alice?"

"She thinks Dodo is in love with me."

Mother paused, exhaling a long-held breath. Something in her eyes turned from watery to solid. They way she hardened was a bit frightening.

"Is he?"

"No! Of course he doesn't love me in that way. He loves me as he loves Edith and Ina. We are friends. He is my Uncle. I love him."

Her sour demeanor hadn't changed at all. This was not how this was supposed to go at all. My plan was to tell Mother about the evil seeds Ina had planted, she would believe me and punish her accordingly. Instead, it seemed I was making it worse.

A knock on the door interrupted us. Mother looked to the door and back down to me.

"Alice, go to your room," she said sternly.

I followed her gaze to the door and knew, somehow I just knew, it was Dodo on the other side.

"It's him, is it not?"

"Alice, I said to go to your room."

"No."

Mother's face became enraged. I shrank a little in response.

"Alice, go to your room *now*!"

I turned and left in the direction of the staircase, but as soon as her back was turned to me, I tiptoed to my hiding space next to the parlor. She did not hear me as I tucked my feet under my dress in the corner. The door opened and Mother escorted Dodo into the parlor with a few small words between them. It was hard to breathe where I was hiding, for the air seemed thick with tension. I stood and crawled closer to the door to get a better view of them.

Mother sat in her usual chair and Uncle was in one facing her. She neglected to offer him the courtesy of tea. Perhaps she was meaning to be rude, or perhaps she did not want a servant to see them as they were and feed further rumors.

"Mr. Dodgson, I think you must know why I've called for you."

"I believe I d-d-do. You wish the girls to have a chaperone while in my c-c-company, and I c-could not agree more with you. They are getting to a d-d-delicate age."

She looked at him in a peculiar way, as if trying to sort out if his ignorance was an act or not. I knew that look. Mother was trying to take his measure. The thing was he was remained a difficult man to quantify.

"That's not the matter with which I am referring."

"Oh?"

"Surely you have heard the rumors floating about Christ Church?"

"I p-p-pay no mind to idle gossip, so no one b-bothers to tell it to me."

"Well, this idle gossip involves you, and half the campus is talking of it."

He looked at her perplexed for a moment, and then softened. "Please, d-d-do not be cross with the girl. She is young, and I fear my affections were misunderstood."

"So you are denying that you kissed Ina? You deny that

you have been using the time you've been spending with our girls as a way to court Ina all this time?"

Dodo looked appalled. "What? N-n-no. Is that the rumor? Oh, heavens."

The look on his face was so sincere, Mother's armor softened.

"You mean to say what Alice said was true? Ina kissed you?"

"Yes. I w-w-would not have said anything for fear of the girl's reputation. I only hoped it was a passing infatuation."

Mother studied her hands for a moment, now folded in the lap of her dress. "And the other rumor? The one about Alice?"

Dodo appeared startled all over again. His face flinched as though physically hit. I must have mimicked his look. There was no rumor about me that I had heard. I wondered if there was one, or if this was something she invented to make him confess another deed.

"What about Alice?"

"Why is it you spend so much time with her?"

Dodo shook his head back and forth slowly. He rubbed his forehead with his fingertips as though he were easing a headache.

"She calms me. When stressed, since I was a b-b-boy, the laughter of children has calmed me. Thinking in riddles and games has always b-been a way to relax my mind. Alice is my little muse of sorts. Children are all lovely, b-b-but Alice is...different. I wish..."

He trailed off and stared blankly forward.

"You wish what?"

"It is silly."

"Tell me," said Mother finding Dodo's eyes with hers.

He met those eyes, so much like mine, and looked deeply into them. For a moment, I thought they could see one another's gaps, the places just behind the eyes, where truth cannot hide itself. They were so entranced with one another, if only for a moment.

"I sometimes wish she...she were my daughter."

Mother sat up in slight alarm. "What do you mean, sir?"

"I mean that I d-d-do come here day after day for the girls, to be their Uncle, but I do also come here for another reason, a reason you haven't guessed. It is a lost cause; therefore, I do not p-p-pursue it past the point of fantasy, but it is there all the same, Mrs. Liddell."

Mother stood then and turned away from him. He stood too, desperation painted across his brow. He was embarrassed, but there was no turning back for him now. His face flushed as vibrantly as Ina's had the night she kissed him.

"I am s-s-sorry for the boldness, but it is you. I never wanted to t-tell you such, but I'd rather you know the truth than believe a lie about me. I am, and have b-b-been for some time, in love with you."

Mother turned on him, her face stricken with pain and confusion.

"I know it is unrequited," he said solemnly and quickly, before she could retort anything.

"I am married," she said, neither confirming nor denying his claim.

"Which is why you and I were always a mere fantasy." He put on his hat and made as though he were going to leave.

"Mr. Dodgson," she said, trying to stop him.

Dodo did stop, his blue eyes gazing at her for some semblance of love. Their light pools of blue went on and on and on. My heart ached for him.

"I...I think it would be best if you did not call on us socially again. This all is already confusing the girls so much. Their reputations...well, it is all we women have."

His face fell, and it was everything I could do not to run to him. "I understand," he said with a silent nod to her.

"I am so sorry." The words came out in a whispered breath, tears forming around her eyes. She lifted her hands to her mouth to hide the pain from escaping there.

"Good day, Mrs. Liddell," said my Dodo.

Before my legs could work again properly, he was gone from the parlor with the front door shut behind him.

"No!" I screamed.

I ran as fast as I could after him, partially blinded with

tears, but Mother caught me before I reached the door. Hard, chest-wracking sobs poured from me as I scratched at her to get free. She wrapped my body in hers and we tumbled to the floor.

"No! You cannot send him away! You just can't!"

Mother held me to her chest and hugged me tightly. She rocked me as though I were a tiny babe. I felt her breath in my hair.

"Hush, my dear. It is for the best, my poor Alice. It is all for the best."

Chapter Thirteen

It was not until December that I saw my Dodo again, and had I known what that meeting would entail, I might have skipped the ordeal altogether. He was finally permitted to visit with the knowledge my mother would be listening keenly to the entire conversation in the adjoining room. There was a gift of great importance he wanted to give to me, and I begged relentlessly until she gave in, her stern demeanor softened by the constant barrage of girlish tears.

I was in the drawing room when he arrived, his hair disheveled about his face from the wind and his jacket over one arm. Mr. Dodgson was just removing his gray-and-black gloves when he saw me across the room, and his face dropped. Where a smile had lived only moments before now sat a dismal frown.

I ignored his reaction because I was so very glad to see him.

"My Dodo!" I cried as I ran across the room, my arms outstretched to embrace him like we had a thousand times before.

He hugged me very quickly and without warmth. I moved to kiss his cheek, and he pulled away from me. My mouth quivered on the verge of a sob. This was not at all how I imagined our reunion. All the warmth I had been craving was being denied.

"Uncle Dodo, am I not allowed a kiss on the cheek?" I asked like a woeful child.

"I am afraid much has changed since last we met."

He seemed grave all of the sudden. I thought perhaps he was just nervous. After all, we had not played together in months. I laughed and smiled to make him feel comfortable again.

"Surely, Uncle, I am not so very changed," I said as I leaned in to kiss his cheek again.

"No Alice, d-d-do-don't."

I stopped immediately and stepped backward to put some real distance between us. It was the stammer more than anything else that halted my attempts. He had never stammered with me. Never. Not with me. He only stammered around adults. I looked into his face, which was now shy and reserved, not the face of my Dodo.

"Perhaps then I am much changed for you to treat me so," I said, my voice betraying my hurt.

"You are, Alice, or I was t-t-too blind to see it b-b-before."

"What is so terrible about me now?" My voice trembled

with the emotion of it all, so much of it I did not understand. He looked up into my eyes. His seemed older somehow and weary.

"You have the look of your mother. I fear you have grown up in these past few months."

The death of silence entered the room and lingered about our heads. I wondered why his look and those words made me feel so strange. The memory of what I had seen those months ago with my mother and Mr. Dodgson flooded my mind, as did the kiss I had seen Ina give him. All swirled around us in such a frenzy that I felt the uncomfortable air fill the room and leave us stifled. Every stammer was a jab in the chest, but every second of silence reminded me of the stammers left unsaid.

"I told Mother the truth. I told her about Ina and what a wicked fish she has been, spreading lies about you. This is all Ina's doing, but Mother would not believe me."

"No Alice, it is my d-d-doing. Your mother was right. I should have known better than t-t-t-to interfere with young ladies' affairs. You and Ina are far t-t-too old for an old b-bachelor like me to visit."

"Do not say that! You are my friend, my Dodo! Please, do not listen to them."

"Alice, d-d-d—"

"And do not stammer with me!" I screamed, tears rolling down my cheeks. "You never stammered with me. We were friends, you and I."

In a fit of exasperation, I ran to him and threw my arms

about his waist. He could throw me off if he liked, but I would hug him first. To my infinite relief, he embraced me back and relaxed under my arms.

"My dear, Alice," he said slowly, trying to keep his stammer in check. "I am so sorry."

We ended our embrace reluctantly and replaced the distance between us. The hug had not ended the awkward feelings, only delayed them for a moment. He still looked at me with that shyness he reserved only for adults, and I was powerless to change it.

"I have a g-gift for you."

Mr. Dodgson reached into his pockets of his coat and produced a small, handmade book. The title was *Alice's Adventures Underground*. I recognized his handwriting and drawings immediately once I opened the book. It was the story he had told us that lovely day in July, the day of fun and rhymes and glasslike water beneath us. I had made him promise to write it down and he had, for me.

"It is a b-b-bit early for Christmas, so it will have to b-be an unbirthday present," he said with a mock-cheerful grin.

His lip quivered with the effort of trying to act at ease. I could tell he was proud of his little book but was trying to be humble. To me, it was a treasure, and I hugged it to my chest. The intense urge to weep welled up inside my throat again. I had to swallow it back down.

"Thank you, Dodo. It is wonderful."

"I am glad you like it," he said sincerely. He then replaced his gloves and began to put on his coat to leave.

"But you must come back soon and read it to me. It just simply is not the same without you to do the voices."

He turned back and looked at me with sorrow in his face. A great weight had filled his head and sat heavily under his eyelids. The hope in my voice was crushed beneath that weight.

"You are not coming back are you?"

"I am not."

Hot tears returned, and I was helpless as they tumbled down my cheeks.

"But why? What have I done?"

He crossed the room and embraced me again. I could smell the crisp scent of the wet snow still melting on his coat. I wept harder in his arms and squeezed his torso. Perhaps, I thought, if I held him tight enough, he would stay.

"Oh my dear girl. You have d-d-done nothing. It is the folly of nature and the foolishness of old bachelors like myself. I will never forget you, my little muse, my Alice."

He released me and kissed my forehead. For a moment we stood there, forehead to forehead, sobbing like children in the drawing room together. Time stood still for but a few minutes, and then he was gone. No goodbye or farewell accompanied his form out of the room. No words from my lips followed him outside like a trailing ghost.

For years, I imagined something I might say after him. Sometimes, if I was in a terrible mood, I thought of nasty things to shout after him. Other times, I imagined beautiful words I could recite from a poem that might turn him around and change his mind. All of it was fancy, of course. The man left that day, and nothing could change the fact that I had said nothing.

I stood there in the room, sobbing into my handkerchief. What more was there to do? My best friend was gone now, never to return, and the reason was beyond me. We did no wrong. Why must we suffer? I clutched my little gift and cried harder. A great tearing sensation burst through my chest, leaving a terrible pain in its wake. This must be what a broken heart feels like, I thought. Of course it was, but it was the first one, and I had never seen its like until that moment.

I sat on a chair and blotted my eyes once my sobbing had begun to ease, yet the sound of crying continued. I looked around the room, but still I found it empty except for myself. Perhaps I had attained a wheeze in my chest or a whistle in my nose without realizing. I held my breath, but the sound continued, faint though it was.

I followed the noise, which was definitely not my own, across the room and to door which lead to the hallway. I opened the door only slightly to seek out the source of the weeping. There sat a small chair, and in it, sat my mother. She wept uncontrollably into her own handkerchief, having heard everything that had happened in the drawing room.

Chapter Fourteen

It was the first one, and they do say the first cuts the deepest. What I never expected was how the first heartbreak would linger so. At every turn in my life, there was my Dodo, there was that moment when we said farewell to the friendship that inspired the books. Yes, my book was later published, under a different name and with pictures of a girl who looked not a thing like me. I always wore my dark hair short with cropped bangs, unlike the long-haired, blond Alice in the illustrations. Even though we never resembled one another, I soon became famous as *the* Alice. A label that first seemed fun, but fun turned to quaint and quaint turned to tiresome so very quickly.

I did hear from Mr. Dodgson from time to time. Mother kept her word, and we were not allowed to accompany him anywhere, nor was he invited to the house. He wrote to me now and again, and I to him. The letters never seemed to matter much, since neither of us knew what to say. We were caught inside a whirlwind, just holding on to our own anchors until it was through. The trick was it was never through.

Mother took most of my letters from him and burned them. Ina's met the fireplace as well. I was told he did the same for my letters and his diary pages. All was offered up to the fire in the name of keeping the family name reputable.

He had told me in a few of the letters that he was working on a sequel to the book, one which would explain a great deal. When it finally was published in 1871, the famous Lewis Carroll sent me an autographed copy. The inscription was to 'My Dear Queen Alice", but of course, it was written backward so one could only read it properly if one held a mirror to the words. It was a favorite game of ours, pretending that the people and things in the mirror were in fact other versions of ourselves in another world. Dodo loved the idea that things made more sense on the other side of the mirror.

I loved the looking glass book, perhaps even more than the original, for one very important character in it. The White Knight was he. My Dodo, for all his stammering flaws, became a knight after all by his own words.

The knight fell from his horse as often as Dodo stumbled in conversation, and he had a number of silly inventions that refused to work, but he was a gallant, silly old thing. No, dear Uncle could not disguise himself that well from me, especially when describing the knight's mild, blue eyes.

The first time I read his part, I wept far more than the

fictional Alice at his song, for it had a deeper meaning than most others knew. He escorted her the very last leg before she reached the place where a little girl would turn into a queen, and he'd see her never again. A funny sort of man who only hoped his little queen would remember him.

And now, if e'er by chance I put

My fingers into glue,

Or madly squeeze a right-hand foot

Into a left-hand shoe,

Or if I drop upon my toe

A very heavy weight,

I weep, for it reminds me so

Of that old man I used to know –

Whose look was mild, whose speech was slow,

Whose hair was whiter than the snow,

Whose face was very like a crow,

With eyes, like cinders, all aglow,

Who seemed distracted with his woe,

Who rocked his body to and fro,

And muttered mumblingly and low,

As if his mouth were full of dough,

Who snorted like a buffalo –

That summer evening long ago,

A-sitting on a gate.

Chapter Fifteen

I know what people whispered, and I never cared. A lot of perversion and nonsense, which is often the stuff that makes up a lesser person's mind. Dodo was a kind soul, a creative one. To try to understand his love of children when not knowing the man is like trying to play chess without knowing the rules of the game. One can project all sorts of meaning on the sculpted pieces in front of them when one doesn't understand what they are for.

Dodo was a sweet soul who never lost the wonderment of childhood. He felt more comfortable around children because they still held all the imagination and wonder that most lost in adulthood. While most saw children as silly things who needn't be taught anything but morals and lessons, he saw them as beautifully innocent beings who could appreciate a good bit of nonsense.

Oh and the Freudians, how I loathed the Freudians. They came into popularity and tore my precious story to ribbons. I heard their perversions and never gave another ounce of attention to them afterward. In my personal opinion, Sigmund Freud was a disgusting man who understood nothing about women or children.

Many pointed to the photographs of the children he knew, some being in the nude, as proof of perversion. I cannot fully explain how much this upset me. In the age I was a child, the nudity of a young child was a pure thing. There was nothing sexual about a child comfortably nude without the knowledge of shame yet marring their image. All of Dodo's child friends were photographed with parental consent and supervision. Certainly, one would be hard pressed to find a parent of means without a nude picture of their young child. Some kept them to embarrass the poor thing later in life, an idea Dodo despised.

Children see no shame in nudity. They haven't learned of it yet. No child looks at their body, however it might be built, and sees something to hide. Therefore, to project any shameful ideas on such an innocent creature says more about the projector than the projected, in my opinion.

Ina was another matter entirely. The Freudians and the journalists could be ignored, as we were accustomed to doing such, but Ina was...volatile. We were always close as sisters were, but the rift that began at Christ Church in 1863 never fully mended. In all honesty, I do not believe she was ever the same either. The girl became an indecisive thing and flighty. She oscillated often between tearful remorse and delusional ramblings. I think she loved Dodo not as an Uncle but as a husband, and the fact he did not love her in return forever altered her disposition.

We never discussed what she had done, nor did any of the parties involved ever divulge what really happened that fateful summer. None of us wanted Ina's reputation to be put into question, and likewise, the many questions about Mother and Mr. Dodgson would need to be buried in a place no one would find.

When we were older, a nosey journalist by the name of Florence Lemon came sniffing around for information. She wanted to know about my relationship with Charles Dodgson, and I told the terrible woman I was ill and couldn't speak with her. Ina, however, did speak with her in one of her ever-present flighty moods. I received a letter from her shortly after, full of remorse and faux shame.

My dear! I begin to tremble at what I said to her. I said his manner became too affectionate to you as grew older, and that Mother spoke to him about it, and that offended him, so he ceased coming to visit. I also told her you were fourteen, and I was eleven at the time, even though looking at our birthdays, she could see it was false. I don't know what's come over me.

Ina's need for his affection apparently never left her.

The decades passed, and the questions rose again and again. It was common knowledge that there was a mysterious rift between our family and Dodo. It was even dubbed the "Liddell Riddle." Mr. Dodgson never married, and the issue of his bachelorhood and child friends was called into question. Often, he was asked about me, and I was constantly asked about the infamous Lewis Carroll. We rarely answered any questions about one another, and we never told the reality, no matter how many times I wanted to.

He wrote to me once, urging me to continue the charade, for the family's sake. People would say and think what they wished, no matter how much we shouted the truth. I promptly burned the letter afterward.

The only correspondence I kept from him was a note attached to a wedding gift. I couldn't tell you what he gave me, I am sure something lovely, but the note was the thing I just never could part with.

I have had scores of child-friends since your time, but they have been quite a different thing.

Chapter Sixteen

I earlier spoke of six heartbreaks required to kill a muse, and thus far, I have only spoken of the first. I suppose it was the one that stuck with me the entirety of my life. Living as the infamous Alice never left me, you see. It could have been worse. I could have been that poor Peter Davies who inspired *Peter Pan, the Boy Who Never Grew Up.* Keeping a wise perspective on life is crucial when you are a muse, for often, people never think we really lived.

When I was twenty, I fell in love, and being who I was, I fell in love with the most unattainable boy I could find. The fact that he was a charming and kind fellow helped matters along. Prince Leopold, Queen Victoria's youngest son, came to Christ Church at Oxford for his undergraduate study. We met and fell madly in love immediately.

He was a kind soul, and we wanted to marry, but the queen wouldn't have it. After all, I was a commoner, and he was royalty. It did not matter that I was the famous

Alice from the books; I was still common. There were rumors that the queen was a great fan of Lewis Carroll, and he sent her letters on my behalf. My Dodo was always quite taken with royalty.

Alas, nothing came of it, and my dear Leopold and I had to say our farewells as far as lovers went. We remained dear friends. He even named his daughter Alice, after me.

That was heartbreak number two. I had never loved a man before my prince, and to make matters worse, he loved me back. And when we cried our farewells in one another's arms, I felt that sickeningly familiar snap inside my chest.

In 1876, it came again to me. This time in the form of Edith. You see, Edith was the small, sweet one of us all. She was everything good and pure in this world. Edith was not spiteful the way Ina could be, nor was she stubborn the way I could be. She was just lovely. A young cricketer had caught her fancy, and they were engaged to be married. When a fever hit her, we thought nothing of it. When the spots appeared, then we worried. All the worrying and prayers in the world did not save my dear sister, the one who was the best of all of us. She died on a warm day in June, and she was my heartbreak number three.

I did marry, lest anyone think my life a torrent of terrible news, to a nice cricketer named Reginald Hargreaves. Did I love him? Yes, I suppose I did in a way.

It wasn't the way I had loved Leopold surely, but it was a respectful and proper love.

I had children of my own, three sons. Two of them died fighting in the Great War. Their deaths were so sudden and close together for me that it felt like one terribly drawn-out heartbreak number four. I do not like to discuss my boys. Some things mothers are just not supposed to live through. For some reason, I was chosen to endure it, so endure I did. It's not what I would have chosen, but no one asked me my opinion. I wanted to go into the ground with them, but in the end, it just was not my way.

When Reginald died in 1926, I mourned him. I wept at his funeral, and I felt sorrow at the loss of him. Yet that old familiar snap in my chest did not happen the way it ought. It was not until two years later when I decided that I had to sell my manuscript, the handwritten book of *Alice's Adventures Underground,* in order to pay Reginald's death duties and keep up our estate, that the terrible old feeling returned.

Sotheby's auctioned that tiny piece of my heart and soul for a phenomenal sum, and when that gavel crashed down for the last time, I felt a crack within my chest. Heartbreak number five wracked my ribcage and left me reeling with memories of that cold day in December when my friend had given me the treasure.

The last time I saw him was at my wedding. At least, I'd like to believe it was him.

My wedding day had been lovely, a great affair in

Oxford. Everyone was there. Well, save one. It was rumored that Mr. Dodgson would not attend. The invitation had been sent despite Mother's warnings against it. We had written here and there throughout the years, keeping up with one another's lives. I had hoped he would come despite it all.

I looked for him all day. It was probably gauche of me to be always craning my neck, like a flamingo, looking for a man who was not my bridegroom, but there it was. We made it through the service, dull as they all go, without a sighting of the infamous Lewis Carroll. There were so many people, it was hard to tell a raven from a writing desk.

It wasn't until the end of the ceremony that I caught a glimpse of that tall hat of his just on the outer rims of the crowd filing out of the church. I stood up taller despite all my finery to catch his gaze. He was walking away from the church in the opposite direction of the crowd. I knew that gait anywhere.

Mother and I were standing next to the wedding carriage. Reginald had already seated himself inside and was offering his hand to help me in to join him. The driver offered his hand as well to help me up the steps of the carriage. I looked to Mother and hastily handed her my bouquet of flowers. I accepted the driver's hand but did not join my new husband inside just yet. Instead, I stood on the steps of the carriage, holding onto the hand rail, to better shout over the crowd gathered around me.

"Dodo!" I called despite the strange stares.

"Alice! Get down from there," scolded Mother from slightly below.

Those blue eyes turned to me with that long hair of his, more silver in it than I remembered, always longer than it was fashionable. He looked into my face, and I smiled like a lunatic and waved to him. He smiled back at me. With a simple nod, the slightest of bows, he tipped his hat to me with those fine gloves of his. And like that, he was gone. The white knight seeing off little Alice, who was now a queen.

Epilogue

"I do not understand why you are being so contrary," Caryl said while finishing his breakfast across from me. He wiped his mouth with his napkin in that exasperated way he did when he was frustrated with me. I looked down at my own breakfast, barely touched and hardly appetizing.

"I'm not being contrary. These Americans do not know how to cook an egg properly," I retorted.

"Mother, you have to eat. Today is a big affair."

"Don't you order me, Caryl. I know perfectly well what today is."

I sipped my tea and ate a bit of toast to ease his glares. At least the toast was edible, even though the tea was merely passable at best.

"I should think you'd be in a better mood. It's not every day Columbia University makes someone an honorary doctor of literature."

I scoffed, nearly spilling my tea.

"A lot of nonsense that is."

"I thought you liked nonsense."

"Don't be cheeky with me. This is altogether the wrong brand of nonsense. I have done nothing of worth. Certainly nothing that would entitle me to a doctorate degree."

"You inspired two of the most influential children's books in history."

"So I'm a doctor of musery, am I? Is there even such a word?"

"Mother, please."

"Stand back all and let Doctor Muse through the hall. Ha, I think not."

He gave up and left to retrieve our hats. I took mine from him and situated it on my head, as was befitting the style of the time. Caryl lowered his hand and helped me to my feet. It was 1932, and I was an old woman, nearly eighty. We were in New York City, a place far too exciting for my liking.

"You will see your book again," he said to me with a smile.

It stopped me short, the thought of it. My book would be there. It was one of the relics on display on this centennial of my Dodo's birth. The other, of course, was me. My dear Dodo wouldn't be there, of course. He had died on January 14, 1898 from pneumonia. So, here I was, accepting a doctorate of musery on behalf of my long-lost friend. I would be lying if I said that I hadn't made the ghastly journey to America because of him. It was of course because of Dodo I was doing this, and to see my book again.

We travelled to Columbia University along the busy streets of New York. I wondered if they were always this busy, or if all the fuss was because of the upcoming ceremony. Such a selfish thought. I was feeling a bit dizzy.

We arrived with a flurry of people around us. Young men and women buzzed about me like flies. I clung to Caryl and my walking cane to hold steady. Someone insisted I wear a graduate's cap and gown to accept my diploma. A lot of stuff and nonsense if you asked me, but no one did, so I complied.

When the time came, President Nicholas Murray Butler stood before the crowd with me on one side and my book, ensconced in glass on a pedestal, on the other. Dodo's original manuscript was to be donated to Columbia University. I eyed the book from across the stage, desperately wanting to see it closer. My hands ached to touch it as though there was an invisible tether between me and its bound pages.

The president's speech was respectful and blessedly short before he announced that Columbia University was bestowing upon me a degree of Doctor of Letters for inspiring the famed books by Lewis Carroll. Everyone applauded as Caryl helped me to my feet. I walked to the center stage and accepted my degree in that ridiculous cap and gown, smiling as was befitting the moment. I was nothing if not proper.

Then, I walked to the book. There, beneath the glass, it sat as I always remembered it. I wanted to say something to it, to possibly caress it one last time. How often had my fingers touched those pages? The edges were worn from years of reading, again and again. I reached out instinctively, still clasping the diploma. If only the glass were to dissolve.

"Mother?"

It was Caryl who broke me out of my reverie. He took my hand and escorted me back to my seat, but my eyes did not leave the book until the porters carried it away. I never saw it again.

I am not a fan of ships. Of course, I am not opposed to them either, as they were a convenient means of transportation. We traveled in luxury, but no amount of money can pay the seas to smooth themselves and cease casting us about our rooms like marbles in a jar. It was a long and grueling voyage. Traveling truly was for the young, I decided.

We arrived at the estate by automobile. I disliked automobiles. They smelled and bounced around in ways a carriage never did, but Caryl insisted. He had also insisted there was to be a surprise for me waiting at the house, and I wasn't to see it until we arrived. For this purpose, he blindfolded me with a silk scarf when we neared the perimeter of the estate.

"I want to see the outer gardens," I protested.

"Mother, you may see them later."

"But I want to make sure the roses are red this time. Last time, that gardener planted white roses, and they were just..."

"We are here, Mother."

"We are?"

The automobile rolled to a stop. I could hear the dirt and rocks break under the tires as they were prone to do, but nothing else was audible. There was something about the air, something unusual. As if a good deal of people were trying ever so desperately to be so quiet they were not breathing. Not even the birds sang.

"Caryl, what have you done?"

"Wait here. I will run around to your side and help you out of the car."

"But..."

I heard his door slam and the sound of footsteps circling the rear of the automobile. The sound of my door opening alerted me to his presence once again. He lifted my blindfold and helped me to step out of the metal beast. There, in front of me was an overwhelming sight.

Red roses covered every stationary surface in view. There were banners hanging from windows with pictures of me as a girl, illustrations of mock turtles, white rabbits in waistcoats, dodos, caterpillars, mad hatters, white knights, and red queens. Flowers of every imaginable color were newly planted along the entranceway. One tremendous banner hung high across the house with the Cheshire cat, his big grin the kind that knew the secret of the world but would never tell it. His banner read a proud message.

Welcome Home to Wonderland, Alice!

All of the servants, scores of my friends and family, and even the cats were gathered outside to welcome me home. Some even dressed the part of the Mad Hatter or the white rabbit. A friend had come with her two grandsons dressed as Tweedle Dee and Tweedle Dum. Caryl had to hold on to me as I became weak in the knees. They repeated what the banner said.

"Welcome home to wonderland, Alice!"

I began to cry then. Old woman tears they were. For so long I had been tired of being Alice from Wonderland, its burden being such a heavy weight for me. But now, I remembered what wonderland really was. Not a fictional place dreamed up by the captain of dreamers. It was a real place that I once called home with my dear friend. I had missed it so.

It was then that he appeared to me. Perhaps I was senile, though I did not feel as such. I wondered if all mad people thought they were sane or if it was the other way around. Mad or sane, he was there at my side in his white knight's armor. He wore no helmet in order to show off his waves of silver-and-white hair. Those mild blue eyes were smiling at me, while the gap beneath them told me volumes about how much he had missed me.

"Welcome home, Alice dear," he said with a slight bow.

"You came. After all this time," I said, tears rolling down my wrinkled face.

"I wouldn't have missed it for the world."

I reached out and touched his cheek, a smile stretching across my face as wide as the Cheshire cat's. It was as warm as I remembered.

"Mother, who are you talking to?" asked Caryl on my other side.

Dodo winked at me, and I knew the game.

"No one, dear. Nobody is here."

Then, the most unexpected thing happened. Somewhere in the old cage of bones and brittle bits that made up my chest, something snapped. An old, familiar pain it was. One I hadn't felt in ages. Unlike its previous incarnation, it did not hurt the way it should've. Perhaps pain was not a prerequisite after all, for I was gloriously happy then, hugging my son in front of everyone I knew. Nonetheless, there it was, like my old friend come to remind me one last time who I really was. This was heartbreak number six, and I could not have been happier to welcome it.

Afterword

There is a question I hear often whenever I write historical fiction, particularly fiction about real people. In this book, the real Alice comes to life to tell a story of great friendship and the heartbreak of a muse. It is my job to weave fiction with fact to create an original story. If the reader cannot see the line between the two, then I have done my job well, but that leaves an important query that must be addressed.

How much is true?

Since this book attempts to fill in the blank parts of history, I feel obliged to draw that line in the sand between what is true and what I fabricated. Please allow me to give you the facts before I explain the fiction.

Charles Dodgson (Lewis Carroll) was indeed a professor of mathematics at Oxford and a deacon of the Anglican Church. The Liddell family lived in the deanery, and they had a very close relationship with Mr. Dodgson. A confirmed bachelor, Charles never married and enjoyed taking on an uncle role with the families he befriended. In a time when photography was still relatively new, he was a skilled photographer who specialized in beautiful photographs of children.

Mr. Dodgson had a special relationship with Alice Liddell and spent a great deal of time with her family. He specialized in fanciful stories and word play, entertaining Alice and her sisters regularly. It has been documented that the boat ride he took with the girls on July 4, 1862 was the day *Alice in Wonderland* was conceived. Alice was in fact his muse, and she received a doctorate of literature from Columbia University for her part in creating this timeless piece of children's literature.

Certain parts of *Alice in Wonderland* have been connected to the real people and things in the Liddell family's life. It is believed that Mr. Liddell was the inspiration for the white rabbit, as he was often running late. In England, ground-up mummified cats were used as fertilizer, but it is in no way connected to the invention of the Cheshire Cat. There are accounts of Victorian children keeping dormice as pets in tea kettles. The Liddell children were the subjects of several characters in the story, and Charles Dodgson was said to the be the dodo on account of his stammer causing the "dodo" part of his name.

Why did he prefer the company of children?

Alice and her sisters were not the only children he befriended as an uncle figure. It was said that at any gathering, Dodgson gravitated to the younger attendees as opposed to speaking with his peers. His preferred photography subjects were also children. This has often been interpreted by modern analysts as evidence of pedophilia. After researching his life, I am skeptical of this conclusion.

Dodgson was the eldest boy of eleven children and grew up entertaining his siblings. For whatever reason, he was uncomfortable around adults. This led to a stammer when speaking with them, but with children, he felt at ease. Perhaps this was the leading factor in his choice to spend a great deal of time with children.

Though he photographed colleagues and other adults, his photography is scrutinized for the age of his most famous models. To modern eyes, it seems unusual that an adult man would seek out children to photograph. However, the photographs he took of children were mostly commissioned by their parents. Much like we would today, parents hired him as a photographer to capture portraits of their families.

As far as the uncle role he took on with the Liddell family, it was common for a bachelor in Victorian times to be adopted by a family and act as an uncle to their children. He was extremely imaginative and invented stories and games for children, much like he did with his own brothers and sisters. His relationship with the Liddell children was nothing unusual for the time period.

It is extremely dangerous to instill modern morals into

history. If one truly wants to understand a person, they must first understand the culture in which they lived. There are a number of things people in Victorian England did that would be considered lunacy today. Often times, people in mourning would create pieces of art from hair. They might take their hair and the hair of the deceased and weave whole sculptures or jewelry with it. It was also normal practice to photograph people who had died and display the pictures. Not to mention, arsenic was ingested and used in makeup because they believed it would keep them looking young.

If a person today were to drink arsenic, photograph dead children, and weave hair jewelry, they would be committed immediately. Yet, in the time of Queen Victoria, these were normal practices.

What really happened with Charles Dodgson and the Liddell family?

This is what most people call "The Liddell Riddle," and to be clear, no one really knows what happened. All those involved never spoke of it, and they took the truth to their graves. Some event occurred that caused a rift between Charles and the Liddells which was never fully repaired. Mr. Dodgson was allowed to give Alice copies of the books she inspired, but he kept his distance from the family.

Many speculate Mr. Dodgson was courting Ina. Although she was fourteen, by Victorian standards she was old enough to have suitors and should have had a chaperone when with him. The flip side of this theory has Ina becoming infatuated with Charles, and the separation that followed was to protect the girl's prospects and reputation. Others think he was interested in the governess or Mrs. Liddell herself. The most scandalous theory was that he had fallen in love with his muse and proposed marriage to Alice. Though she was only eleven, girls of twelve or thirteen were considered of age to marry at that time.

No documents give a hint as to what happened, and the pages covering the days of June 27-29 of 1863 were ripped from Charles Dodgson's diary. Only Ina broke the silence, talking to a journalist later in her life. Much of what she said was called into question when she penned a remorseful letter to Alice after her interview professing to have given false information for reasons she couldn't identify. Unfortunately, any so-called truths about the "Liddell Riddle" remain supposition. It is anyone's guess as to what really happened.

I cannot profess to be an expert regarding the life of Charles Dodgson and Alice Liddell. My version of events is complete fiction. I have no secret insight whatsoever into Ina's infatuation or Charles Dodgson's love for Mrs. Liddell. There is no evidence that proves or disproves my version of the "Liddell Riddle." This was the version of history that blossomed in my mind while researching two amazing people who created something magical together. I crafted the story I wanted to tell.

About the Author

Michelle Rene is a creative advocate and the author of a number of published works of science fiction, historical fiction, humor and everything in between. You may have also seen her work under the pen names Olivia Rivard and Abigail Henry. She has won several indie awards for her historical fiction novel, *I Once Knew Vincent.*

Michelle's favorite places in the world are museums, galleries, and libraries. Everyone who creates tells a story of some kind or another. Whether she's painting, writing, or making a video game, Michelle is dedicated to her obsession with storytelling.

When not writing, she is a professional artist and all around odd person. She lives as the only female, writing in her little closet, with her husband, son, and ungrateful cat in Dallas, Texas.

Other Books by Michelle Rene

Tattoo: A young woman appears in a cynical post-Judgement Day age, and a band of strangers who find themselves called to keep her safe.

Hour Glass: Set in the lawless town of Deadwood, South Dakota, Hour Glass shares an intimate look at the woman behind the legend of Calamity Jane told through the eyes of twelve-year-old Jimmy Glass.

I Once Knew Vincent: Maria was a poor girl trying to keep her alcoholic mother alive until the day Vincent stepped into her life and changed it forever. Before he was the infamous artist, Vincent Van Gogh was her friend.

About the Publisher

Annorlunda Books is a small press that publishes books to inform, entertain, and make you think. We publish short writing (novella length or shorter), fiction or non-fiction. Our publication criteria are simple: if we like it and it taught us something new or made us think, we'll publish it.

Find more information about us and our books online at annorlundaenterprises.com/books/, on Facebook at facebook.com/annorlundabooks/, or on Twitter at @AnnorlundaInc.

To stay up to date on all of our releases, subscribe to our mailing list at annorlundaenterprises.com/mailing-list/

Selected Other Titles
from Annorlunda Books

Original Short eBooks and Collections

Both Sides of My Skin, by Elizabeth Trach, is a collection of short stories exploring the reality of pregnancy and motherhood.

The Burning, by J.P. Seewald, is a novella set in the coal country of Pennsylvania, about a family struggling to cope as a slow-moving catastrophe threatens everything they have..

The Inconvenient God, by Francesca Forrest, is a fantasy novelette about a government official tasked with retiring a god who isn't quite ready to leave.

The Lilies of Dawn, by Vanessa Fogg, is a fantasy novelette about love, duty, family, and one young woman's coming of age.

Water into Wine, by Joyce Chng, is a sci-fi novella about a family trying to build a life amidst an interstellar war that threatens everything.

Caresaway, by DJ Cockburn, is a near future "inside your head" thriller about a scientist who discovers a cure for depression, but finds that it comes at a terrible cost.

Unspotted, by Justin Fox, is the story of the Cape Mountain Leopard, the scientist dedicated to saving these rare and elusive big cats, and the author's own journey to try to see one.

Okay, So Look and *Here's the Deal*, by Micah Edwards, are humorous, accurate and thought-provoking, retelling of The Books of Genesis and Exodus.

Don't Call It Bollywood, by Margaret E. Redlich, is an introduction to the world of Hindi film.

Academaze, by Sydney Phlox, is a collection of essays and cartoons about the tenure track and beyond at a research university.

Taster Flights

Hemmed In is a collection of classic short stories about women's lives.

Love and Other Happy Endings is a collection of classic short love stories that all end on a high note.

Missed Chances is another Taster Flight of classic stories about love and "the one that got away."

Small and Spooky is a collection of classic ghost stories that feature a child. These stories are spooky with a hint of sweet.

CPSIA information can be obtained
at www.ICGtesting.com
Printed in the USA
BVHW081141130921
616662BV00004B/292